*To the Tri-Cities Historical Museum
for preserving the memories.*

*And to The Bookman
for sharing the word.*

Grand Haven: a historical mythology.

Miller, Nelson.

Crown Management, LLC – July 2024

1527 Pineridge Drive
Grand Haven, MI 49417
USA

ISBN-13: 979-8-89292-863-2

All Rights Reserved
© 2024 Crown Management, LLC

1

Again. He'd done it again. How many times would he make the same mistake, plunging down the same rabbit hole? Repeatedly, beating his head against the same wall, his mood despairing, despondent.

Maroon hadn't been happy in a long time. He'd nearly forgotten what happiness is. The odd thing was, Maroon lived in Grand Haven. How could one not find happiness in a place with a name like *that*? His life, though, didn't feel grand. Nor did he feel as if he lived in any kind of a haven.

Oh sure, Grand Haven was a gorgeous place. It had all the charm of a seaside town, rooted firmly in the Upper Midwest buckle of the Bible Belt. The *Wall Street Journal* had once touted the town as the *Hamptons of the Midwest*, to the chagrin of locals who knew that the national notoriety would soon change the town. It did, but not enough to spoil it.

Maroon had lived in Grand Haven for what, thirty years? Forty years? Too long to remember. He should have thanked his lucky stars. When his work colleagues in Grand Rapids, Lansing, and Detroit learned of his lakeshore residence, they uniformly reminded Maroon of his good fortune. Grand Haven was where they *visited*, a place to which they would consider themselves fortunate to *retire*, not where they *lived* while they worked.

But as much as Maroon had been glad to move to Grand Haven so long ago, and as much as he sacrificed in commutes, career advancement, and professional connections by doing so, Maroon hadn't found himself happy. He lived in a grand haven, to be sure, but not one that promoted his happiness.

The one thing that Maroon had learned, living in both the literal and figurative Grand Haven, was that happiness wasn't a matter of place. Happiness might be a matter of a lot of things, like peace, security, health, relationship, and provision. But if place was part of the formula, it must be a smaller part, certainly not the whole enchilada or the enchilada's protein ingredient.

Maroon spent a good deal of time looking for other things to blame for his generally somber mood, far more down and weighted than his favored geographic location and its gorgeous natural environment seemed to warrant. He found plenty of niggling things to credit. Irritants were frequent, no doubt, flaring up several times a day.

But that was exactly the problem. The things Maroon could legitimately say were wrong in his life were so small as to be inconsequential. They were *first world problems* at most, indeed more likely problems with his own character and capacity for dealing with the world. The things that bothered him shouldn't, he knew. And that they *did* bother him just made him all the more irritable.

Maroon got up from his desk to take a walk, out the back through the spectacular cemetery tucked among the old-growth-forest dunes piled up along the lakeshore. The town's founders from the 1830s had buried their dead in what was now the downtown square—not a good look for a modern tourist town. Fortunately, in the 1880s the town's leaders took stock of the town's growth surrounding the growing central cemetery. They cleared several hundred acres of forest from the nearby rolling dunelands, laying out a cemetery park to which they laboriously moved the downtown graves, without disturbing any ghosts. The spectacular cemetery park entertained the town's families every summer Sunday after church, each gathering at their heralded plots.

Maroon harrumphed for the umpteenth time as he passed the most extravagant of the family plots. *What a wasted expense,* Maroon thought. The grand family plots had been empty of Sunday celebrants for decades, from the looks of them.

Yet even as he considered with disdain the families' foolishness, Maroon heard a whisper of conscience that perhaps the families had been of better spirit than him. At least they had found something to celebrate, something to gather them in celebration, even if only in memory of their ancestors. He shook his head, though, banishing the thought.

Taking his familiar loop through the cemetery, Maroon paused at some old concrete steps leading up onto a small overlook, deep in the woods. A long time had passed since he'd walked up those old, worn, moss-covered steps. *Why not?* Maroon thought. He turned aside to slowly mount the uneven steps, working their way at an angle up the hillside out of the bright sunshine and into the sylvan half light.

Maroon's heart pounded and head swam with effort as he reached the overlook, shrouded in old growth beech, maple, and oak. He stopped to catch his breath. A glance around reminded him how sparse but magnificently adorned were the old graves, the very graves of the town's handful of founders, atop the overlook.

Time had robbed the overlook of its significance. It had once stood looking down on the splendid plots of the richest families, judging by the height and elaborate nature of the memorials. But the woods had filled in around the overlook. The graves of the town's founders were now an afterthought, entirely hidden from the view of the runners, bikers, strollers, dog walkers, and few gravesite visitors the spectacular cemetery attracted.

Maroon shook his head, letting out a small huff at how time had forgotten even these adventurers who had floated down nearly the full length of Lake Michigan from Fort Mackinac to the mouth of the Grand River, to found Grand Haven as a site for a land and lumber enterprise.

Maroon moved slowly from grand memorial to memorial, reading the names of the founder and his family, including his wife, her brother and sister, and other family members who had joined them in the tiny settlement.

Standing in the woods atop the overlook, Maroon peered out between the trunks and branches toward the bright sunlight from which he had come. He realized that the home office from which he carried on his writing craft looked across a couple hundred yards of green rolling cemetery at the town founders' forest-hidden overlook. He could see his office window out which he frequently looked at the gorgeous cemetery.

Maroon shook his head in brief wonder at his fortunate circumstance. He knew that no one else in town had the view he did of the forest-encircled, dune rippled cemetery, hidden like a jewel in the middle of the grown town.

Maroon had once picked up a book of Michigan's natural wonders. Thumbing through it for what it might name as a West Michigan wonder, he came upon the very cemetery along which he lived. Yes, his work colleagues were right that he lived in an enchanted town. They had no idea, though, just how enchanting was the location of his particular residence within the town where he had the acknowledged privilege to live.

Maroon took a deep breath, for the moment not in a heavy sigh but instead in a bit of refreshing wonder. Could it be? A glimmer of happiness? But no, it was time to get back. Maroon turned from the sylvan overlook toward the steps at its edge.

"Good place to linger, isn't it?" a voice breathed easily into Maroon's ear.

Maroon jumped. He turned slowly toward the voice, still cowering slightly from the startle, bent and ready to run with the adrenaline rush of its lingering instinctual fear.

"I'm sorry," the figure standing just behind and to the side of Maroon added in an easy but apologetic voice, "I didn't mean to startle you."

The odd figure, bearded, small, worn but noble, and in dress too formal to be of this generation, added, "It always happens that way. Not sure what to do about it."

Maroon shook his head, asking, "What?"

"Your startled response," the figure said with a broader but still-apologetic smile, knowing that Maroon was still trying to collect his wits.

Maroon nodded blankly, indeed trying to find a script for the surprise encounter. But the figure was already supplying the script, as he knew he would need to do so.

"Want to chat?" the figure asked politely, motioning toward a low, algae-covered concrete bench arranged to view one of the few grand memorials atop the wooded overlook.

"About what?" Maroon asked, not moving.

Maroon hadn't intended any affront in response to the figure's kind offer. But Maroon was still nonplussed by the figure's sudden appearance and now, more so, by Maroon's growing sense from the figure's dated appearance that he was not exactly of this world.

Maroon tried to recall whether the *Feast of the Strawberry Moon* event was scheduled for town that weekend, enabling visitors to explore the history of the area's Native-American culture, French exploration, English colonization, and American settlement of West Michigan. But no, he didn't think so. And the figure in front of him seemed too authentic and far too out of place deep in the cemetery woods to be play acting.

"Anything that interests you," the figure answered Maroon's question. With a small shrug, the figure turned and walked to the mossy bench. Easing himself down to a seat on it, he exclaimed, "That's better for weary legs."

Maroon's own legs suddenly felt wearier than they had. Mimicking the figure's small shrug, Maroon moved cautiously to the seat on the bench alongside the figure. As Maroon did so, the figure closed his eyes, tipped back his head, took a deep breath, and said with a slow shake of his head back and forth, "What a beautiful place this is."

The figure's comment turned Maroon's mind from the oddity of the encounter to the beauty of the glen. The overlook indeed sat above one of the older parts of the cemetery where the grandest memorials stood. But huge, encircling, tree-covered dunes towered above the overlook, making the overlook feel more like a small plateau near the bottom of a great ravine. A pileated woodpecker's prehistoric call reverberated across the overlook, accentuating the spot's other-worldly nature.

Maroon adjusted his seat to glance at the figure seated beside him. The figure opened his eyes to return the glance with another knowing smile, rightly sensing it was time for introductions.

"My wife and I fell in love with this place the first time we set eyes on it," the figure began. Looking away from Maroon to scan the great dune and huge trees sheltering them from the bright sun, the figure continued, "It was her idea to call it *Grand Haven*."

The figure paused, letting Maroon digest the inference of the figure's identity, before continuing.

"We came down on our ship, the *Supply*, with everything we needed to settle. Mackinac had been good to us, but we needed a fresh start, with our growing family."

Maroon was well aware that Reverend William Ferry and his wife Amanda White Ferry, whose memorials and remains sat atop the overlook site, had come down from their mission outpost on Mackinac Island in the Straits of Mackinac between Lakes Huron and Michigan. Maroon recalled that the year had been 1834.

"How did it go for you?" Maroon heard himself saying, even as he thought how preposterous it was that he had accepted the figure's suggested identity.

Ferry smiled broadly, amused that Maroon was already playing along, before answering, "Oh, it went well. It went well. Sons grew up to run the businesses."

Maroon hadn't recalled much more than that Reverend Ferry succeeded in settling Grand Haven, navigating the rich river mouth and surviving its challenging winters to take advantage of its sheltered harbor, sand hills, and abundant hardwoods and other resources.

At the moment, Maroon didn't recall any details of the patriarch's grand arrival. In fact, as Maroon would later confirm through research, Reverend Ferry and his family landed at their new home in late October, not the best time of year to start a new homestead. Fortunately, fur trader Rix Robinson welcomed Ferry and his family at his log cabin, where within days Ferry would hold the first church service at the site. By the next spring, Ferry had hewn his own log residence out of the abundant hardwoods. A church and frame house would soon follow.

Trade with the area's Ottawa, Chippewa, and Potawatomi tribes helped bridge the gap into the lumbering, land, and mercantile businesses Ferry and his brother-in-law Nathan White soon established. The Native Americans, collectively known as the *People of the Three Fires*, were likely descendants of the Hopewell mound builders who had populated the region two millennia earlier, around the time of Christ.

The *People of the Three Fires* tribes, who also called themselves *The Original People*, thrived in the resource-rich area, hunting, fishing the great Grand River and its tributaries, gathering fruits and berries, and even farming. Soon, though, the 1821 Treaty of Chicago opened the lands south of the Grand River to settlement. By the time Reverend Ferry brought his family to the river's mouth in 1834, settlers were pushing the native tribes further north of the Grand River.

Anytime Maroon thought of Grand Haven's settlement, he recalled his wife's story of finding abundant arrowheads in the sand behind her parents' new home, the first modern residence built in a neighborhood atop the last line of dunes before the town's land flattened out. His wife was born in Grand Haven.

Ferry stopped short in his account, though, wanting instead to turn the conversation to his new friend.

"How's it going for you?" Ferry asked Maroon, giving Maroon a sideways glance before looking back out across the sylvan overlook.

Maroon shrugged. How could he have any perspective on his own life, matching in any way the perspective the historic figure seated next to him could share? Anything Maroon might say would sound trite, far too in-the-moment. The ridiculousness of the conversation began to overwhelm Maroon. He half thought of getting up to march off. But perceiving Maroon's issue, Ferry jumped in to save him.

"I know," Ferry answered Maroon's shrug. Reading Maroon's mind, Ferry continued, "It's hard to get any perspective when you're still living it."

Ferry smiled, pleased at his quip. Maroon found himself nodding in agreement, although now feeling even more overwhelmed at the fact and direction of their conversation.

"Tell you what," Ferry perked up, "You think about it, and we'll talk again later."

Maroon once again nodded. He could firmly tell now that he had absolutely nothing he could have said. He was tongue tied, at a complete loss for words or even thoughts. The whole encounter was far too surreal. And Ferry could tell Maroon was losing it.

"Just one more thing, though," Ferry said, "Thanks for taking care of my church."

Maroon nodded again, dumbfounded but still having a slight sense of Ferry's meaning. Maroon had indeed been an elder and officer of the Presbyterian church Ferry had founded, still thriving in Grand Haven nearly two-hundred years later. Yet Maroon closed his eyes and lowered his swimming head into his hands, feeling as if he might pass out.

When Maroon opened his eyes, Ferry was gone.

2

What a night, Maroon groaned as he rolled out of bed in the predawn darkness.

Maroon had gone to bed early, even earlier than his habit. He had hoped to reflect on his encounter with Ferry, or his vision, dream, imagining, or whatever it was that had happened on the hidden cemetery overlook early in the day. He'd been too busy for the rest of the day with calls, chores, errands, and other distractions to give it any thought, when he knew it needed deep thinking. Or he'd been too shocked by the otherworldly encounter to even consider it while going through the motions of another ordinary day.

Yet Maroon realized Ferry had been right. Maroon needed to get a perspective on things. He needed the long view of his life. What would he say to Ferry when–*if*–he saw him again? Indeed, what would Maroon say to someone if he came back to visit Grand Haven 150 years from now, as Ferry had done—or seemed to do, depending on whether Maroon had just imagined the whole thing? Maroon wanted an answer. He *needed* an answer.

But instead of mulling his overlook encounter in the quiet isolation of his bedroom, Maroon had fallen immediately asleep. And while asleep, he had dreamed.

For Maroon to dream was nothing unusual. Indeed, most nights he dreamt. And most nights, he dreamt desperate dreams. It was not unusual for Maroon to wake in the middle of the night out of breath from the struggle to avoid some terrifying end within one of his nightmares. His nightmares were like a catalog of horrors from stabbings, shootings, and dismemberment to possession or consumption by all sorts of demons.

Maroon had ordinary sorts of night terrors, too, like not being prepared for a school examination, missing a train or plane, not being able to shout a warning to a close family member, or being swept out to sea by a great wave crashing far inland. But just as often, he would awake at the last moment before his horrible demise at the hands, mouth, or dark spirit of some extraordinary evil. Running or trying to run and hiding or trying to hide from shooters, stabbers, and deadly beasts was a common theme.

Yet this night, Maroon hadn't dreamt of his demise or consumption. He had instead dreamed a dream from his childhood, one that was equally terrifying if not nearly so graphic in its terror. Indeed, that was the odd thing about the dream: it was set in a plain, white, empty background, like a movie screen gone blank of anything but the bright light of the projector's bulb. Maroon wasn't even in a body. He was instead just present in mind.

A thin, black line stretched taut across the white screen, without beginning or end. And moving slowly along the line was a great carcass of detritus, some twisted and purposeless amalgamation of cast-off things that the line pierced, supported, and transported.

The white air buzzed or vibrated with tension, suggesting that the formless entity was about to break the string or bring about some other untold cataclysm. But it never did.

Maroon had dreamt the dream repeatedly as a child, never with any variation in anything other than intensity. He had awoken then, as he awoke now, in simple terror of the awful depiction, sometimes in breathless terror, for the creeping image seemed to suck out the very last air.

Maroon had considered the dream often as he matured. Over decades, he had come to conclude that it represented an awful nihilism with which he had become too familiar too early in his life. Maroon couldn't discern how his young spirit had picked it up, although it seemed to shimmer around him like brilliant, dry, desert air, its high-pitched whine telling him that everything was pointless. Reading Kierkegaard, Nietzsche, Sartre, Camus, and Turgenev, alone as a youth, as hand-me-downs from his older brother's college courses, had confirmed what his childhood dream had taught him.

Maroon's maturity had chased his nihilist dream to the margins. The demands of growing up and earning a living, eventually in a professional practice, gave body to the white screen's incorporeal fears. He acquired demons to populate the dream's empty atmosphere. The new nightmare was avoiding the demons.

Maroon thought of these things as he dressed for an early morning bike ride along the lakefront, up the channel boardwalk, along the downtown waterfront, and out across the Third Street bridge to Harbor Island. He made sure to clip on the bike's tiny headlamp and taillight, their batteries charged overnight. He could easily navigate in the darkness from streetlights and moonlight, but his concern was for the lone vehicle that might not see him.

Within minutes, though, Maroon had made his way out to the island, without encountering a single vehicle in the predawn darkness mist. It wasn't truly raining. A heavy mist just hung in the air, likely one that would burn off quickly with the imminent sunrise. Maroon made note to be careful of turning too quickly on the wet pavement, lest the bike's narrow tires slip out from under him. He had once taken a bad early morning spill out on the island, skidding in sand on a bend in an asphalt path. He didn't want a repeat performance.

As Maroon crossed the Third Street bridge over a small channel off the Grand River, he chased two deer off the end of the bridge and onto the nearest reaches of the island. Such a sighting was common. He guessed that the deer meandered into town overnight to munch on gardens, returning across the bridge to the island wilds in the early morning before dawn. Maroon had even grown accustomed to expecting the deer so that they did not startle him.

Soon, Maroon was heading out to the boat launch on the farthest reaches of the island. As he did so, he kept an eye out for other wildlife. His bike had once come upon a fox along a part of the asphalt path hard up against some deep undergrowth. The encounter had been so close that bike and fox hadn't the time to discern the identity of the other, causing more of a brief skirmish than either would have preferred.

When walking the island in the early morning pitch black, Maroon had also once been stalked by a German shepherd, so silently that it had touched or nipped at his glove. Having no idea yet of what dark entity was after him, Maroon's instant recoil and holler had alerted the dog's owner, on the far side of the island's large field. The owner's commands had helped Maroon identify the beast as it slunk off in the owner's direction.

Other than deer, fox, and an occasional dog, the wildlife was mainly turtles, muskrat or beaver, a coyote, raccoon, possum, and then waterfowl, tons of waterfowl. Harbor Island held a cornucopia of wildlife, right on the edge of town, hard along the major highway through town. Maroon wondered how many other towns had such bountiful natural habitat so near their downtown, commercial, and industrial environs.

The lakefront, waterfront, and island environments soon had their salutary effect, clearing Maroon's mind of his childhood-throwback nightmare. On these early morning bikes and hikes, Maroon often listened to podcasts, hours and hours of podcasts, mostly on spiritual, theological, philosophical, psychological, and literary or storytelling matters. But not this morning, when he had intended instead to reflect on his previous day's encounter.

Maroon never quite had the chance.

"Hey!" a voice called to Maroon as he navigated his bike around the perimeter of the large parking lot at the boat launch on the island's farthest reach, alongside the river's main channel.

Maroon snapped his head up from his deepening reflections. Who had called him? Not a single car, truck, or boat trailer dotted the parking-lot expanse, dimly lit in the blackness by just two or three strategically posted perimeter streetlights.

"Hey!" the voice called again, a little louder and nearer.

This time, sitting up on his bike, Maroon saw a figure beckoning him from a spot among the cattails along the parking lot's western flank, where the asphalt slowly sank into weeds and then swamp. Letting his bike coast, Maroon scanned the lot again for a vehicle, scooter, wagon, or other form of transport, wondering both how the figure had gotten there and whether Maroon might find some security or risk from the presence of unseen others. It appeared they were alone.

Letting his bike drift slowly under one of the streetlights in the figure's direction, Maroon examined the figure. Instantly, Maroon sensed something distinct about the figure's simple dress, kind demeanor, and noble stance, much as he had when encountering Ferry on the cemetery overlook the prior day. Could it be Ferry so soon again?

Yet no, this figure was slightly taller and leaner than Ferry had been. And this figure dressed not like an adventurous minister but more like a trapper and woodsman. He wore leather leggings, a looser leather top, and what looked to be moccasins.

As Maroon's bike drifted to a stop a few safe feet short of the figure, Maroon caught sight of rustic gear, including a leather satchel and a staff with a hook and spear on the end, hidden among the tall weeds. The items tended to confirm Maroon's impression that he had happened upon a hunter, fisherman, or trapper, even if one quite distinct from the sportsmen he had seen out on these farthest reaches of Harbor Island, usually with a fancy pickup truck nearby.

"Wait a minute. You're Maroon," the figure said with a broadening smile, as the two stared at one another in the dim light.

Stunned, Maroon nodded. He had no idea what else to do.

"Ferry told me about you," the figure explained, adding, "I didn't expect to see you so soon, though."

Of course, to Maroon it wasn't much of an explanation. Maroon hadn't yet processed his prior day's encounter, if he would ever process it. But the figure's words nevertheless did the trick, giving Maroon the necessary context for whatever conversation or event was about to ensue. He had no reckoning for these weird encounters, other than the reckoning they made of one another, which, Maroon realized later, is a reckoning of sorts. Two historic figures, not one, populated his increasingly enchanted world.

Maroon stood silently balancing astride his bike, like the strange encounter the day before, not knowing what to say or do.

"I was going to chase you off so you didn't disturb the game," the huntsman said sheepishly.

Both Maroon and the huntsman scanned the parking lot's perimeter. A bright sliver of dawn was appearing in the east.

"So, tell me how you're doing," the noble huntsman suggested.

"Well," Maroon replied hesitantly, "That's the same thing Ferry asked. But you and I haven't quite had a proper introduction yet."

"Oh, I'm so sorry," the huntsman replied, "You're completely correct. I just figured...."

The huntsman's voice trailed off as he shook his head.

"Well, never mind," the huntsman resumed, adding, "Let's just say I was here to welcome Ferry and his family when they arrived."

Maroon gave a nodding smile of recognition, replying, "I figured so. You're Rix Robinson."

Maroon knew from a broad curiosity a little of the personal history of the man who preceded Ferry in settling Grand Haven. Robinson, like Maroon, had trained for law. But an unwillingness to surrender to conscription in the War of 1812, and a hefty fine and arrest warrant that followed, led Robinson westward from his Massachusetts birthplace and New York residence. Although well read in law and Shakespeare, Robinson was also an avid huntsman.

Working from the Mackinac Island base of John Jacob Astor's American Fur Company, which Astor planned to challenge the Hudson Bay Company for the Midwest fur trade, Robinson acquired or developed outposts in Grand Haven and up the Grand River, including in what is now Grand Rapids. At ease among the area's Indians, he married Flying Cloud, the daughter of the main chief of the Pere Marquette Indians. When Flying Cloud died after bearing Robinson a son, he married River Woman, the granddaughter of the main chief of the Grand River Indians.

Robinson's marriages, to which he was deeply devoted, and his abundant bundles of fine fur, proved that he had gained the trust and trade of the area's Native Americans. When that trade slowed due to excessive hunting and trapping, Astor's company sent Reverend Ferry and his family to settle Grand Haven, hoping to turn the company from Indian trade to land and lumbering. Robinson welcomed Ferry, forming his own land settlement and mercantile company with Ferry's brother-in-law White.

Although an avid huntsman and most comfortable in the wilds, Robinson would proceed to government prominence, transporting coaches of tribal chiefs to Washington, D.C., to negotiate and sign treaties opening the state's Lower Peninsula to settlement. Robinson became a state senator and advocate for women's suffrage and property rights. He could have been the state's governor but for his Native American wife River Woman to whom he remained devoted until his 1875 death. She died a year later.

"See, you knew me all the time," Robinson replied with a chuckle. He continued, "And you're right. That would be just the sort of thing Ferry would ask, that you tell him how you're doing. Ever the minister, you know?"

Maroon nodded and then shrugged. He didn't really know Ferry, but he knew a little of ministers. And yes, a minister might ask how a parishioner or even a stranger was doing, with more intent than lies in the usual greeting.

"Tell you what," Robinson resumed, "Don't bother giving any account of yourself. There's too much of that going on in the world, you know?"

Maroon nodded, this time not dumbly but instead genuinely catching and agreeing with Robinson's astute assertion. Maroon had the sense that he had been overly focused on himself in an unhealthy way, constantly taking stock of his mental state. Robinson, though, was already moving on with his thoughts.

"I bet Ferry kept saying how beautiful this place is," Robinson surmised, to which Maroon smiled another nod.

"See," Robinson confirmed, "That's another taking stock of one's own reckoning, giving account of one's own reaction to things. I say we do far too much of that."

Sensing that it was his turn to move their peculiar predawn conversation forward, Maroon ventured, "So what do you do instead?"

"That's it, exactly," Robinson agreed, although Maroon hadn't thought he'd asserted any premise. Maroon had instead asked a question. But Robinson explained.

"It's a matter of doing, not thinking, I'd say. See, Ferry's wife named this place *Grand Haven*, as if it was something to regard, a place to assess as enjoyable, as more than sufficient. But for me, this place just sustained me, allowing me to draw from it while it drew from me. You know what I mean?"

Even as he asked Maroon's assent to his assessment, Robinson looked off toward the sliver of sun in the east, ready to send its first thin shafts of light across Harbor Island. But Maroon did know what Robinson meant. And Robinson seemed to know Maroon knew.

"This place has sustained you, too, hasn't it?" Robinson asked, turning his gaze back from the eastern glow to regard Maroon, still astride his bike, hands on the handlebars, feet on the ground.

Maroon nodded. He hadn't thought of it that way, but Grand Haven had indeed supplied his needs, while the town had drawn its needs from Maroon, in a sort of sacralized symbiosis.

Maroon wasn't a huntsman. He didn't trap, shoot game, or even fish. He didn't kayak, canoe, sail, or motor down the channel and out onto the big lake, like many of his acquaintances. But the town had supplied his needs nonetheless, while his work and volunteering had supplied a return, caring for the needs of other locals.

"Look," Robinson said, stirring for the first time since Maroon had pulled up on his bike, "I've got to finish up my hunt. Could you just avoid the perimeter in your circuit, so as not to chase off the game?"

"Of course," Maroon replied, nodding. But he had another thought, adding, "Anything I can tell Ferry, if I see him again?"

Robinson chuckled quietly before replying with a wave of his arm across the island's expanse, "Sure. Tell him to stop thinking so much. Better to just live honestly among these riches."

Maroon nodded, but Robinson had already stooped to gather his gear at his feet. Taking the cue, Maroon mounted his bike and pushed off. As soon as seated securely, he turned to give Robinson a wave or salute goodbye, but Robinson had disappeared without a trace. Curious, Maroon turned his bike in a small loop to carry him back to the place where Robinson had stood among the cattails just a moment before. Nothing. Not a trace.

Maroon huffed silently to himself, shook his head, and pedaled off across the parking lot's brightening tarmac.

3

Maroon mulled Robinson's counsel on his ride back home, as the rising sun's long streaks lit the channel and lakefront. Maroon liked Robinson's tip to think less and live more, drawing your needs from your place while allowing your place to draw its needs from you. Maroon resigned himself to reducing his constant self-assessment, so much or little as he could.

In doing so, Maroon recognized that he might need to shut out or reduce some of the stimuli that urged and fueled that self-attention. That little screen in his pocket was one such culprit. Nearly the whole of the advertising industry, pouring itself out through that little screen, depended on driving that self-attention. The drug ads were the worst. As beneficial as the drugs may be in curing disease, the stories they told seemed less of cure and more of self-realization. But the ads for food, drink, transportation, mortgages, and everything else weren't much different. The goal was self-fulfillment, through some product or service transaction.

Maroon of course realized that he should be thinking about these absurd appearances of historical characters, Ferry first and then Robinson, as much or more so than the conversations they engendered. But he had recognized already the day before, after Ferry's visit, that he could do little to nothing for their comprehension. Maroon might be either delusional, possessed, or dead. But what difference did it make? And so Maroon chose instead to focus on the conversations' content.

Ferry had suggested Maroon account for himself, recognizing the beauty of the place in which he lived. Robinson suggested taking less account, even of anything so abstract as beauty, but to live more deeply in exchange with the rich environment that enabled it. Both suggestions seemed like good counsel. Maybe they were not as opposed as they seemed.

Robinson's soft counsel to live richly engaged in one's environment confirmed for Maroon a direction his thinking had been heading for some time. He had come to realize, through a certain line of reading and listening to certain speakers, that he had spent his life viewing creation through an artificial lens rather than taking it on its own terms. Robinson seemed to be saying the same thing: cast aside one's lens for creation itself of which one is, in the creator's image, the prime point and part.

Maroon, for instance, had gradually relearned to see trees as trees, rather than as their chlorophyll-fueled, oxygen-generating functions, a process he could not see. He could see that trees pointed up and spread out, drawing on the thin or rich soil in which their seeds landed, symbols of humankind itself. Maroon had likewise relearned to see water as wet and delicious rather than as H_2O capable of hydrolyzing acids. In Maroon's recaptured world, a beneficent sun could rise in the east and set in the west, as Maroon experienced it, rather than be an unimaginably large and growing gas ball that would incinerate the earth in a future so distant that it, too, was unimaginable.

Maroon reckoned that both Robinson and Ferry, each in their own way, might be urging Maroon along his phenomenological path toward a natural and integrated experience of his own life. These were the reflections Maroon gained in quiet moments spread through his busy day, after his return home from his Harbor Island encounter with Robinson.

Maroon slept that night without dreams. He nevertheless awoke burdened more than ever. Maroon had never been a cheerful morning person. That he often awoke to sounds of his wife cheerfully cooing at their dogs always filled him with wonder. Who could be so cheerful so early in the morning darkness?

Maroon's own darkness gradually dissipated most mornings, usually by the time he had done his first writing. He could at least be civil a half hour into his pending writing assignments. An hour in, he could be cordial. Two hours in, and he was often glowing with the energy that accomplishment, even such little accomplishment as generating several pages of fresh text, naturally fuels.

This day, though, Maroon awoke in such a dark mood that he knew almost instantly that it wouldn't wear off with the energy of the morning. On these days, he usually went quietly about his way, trying not to be so surly as to offend anyone, even though he felt like it. He could tell that this day would be harder than most to avoid such offenses.

Maroon had always been moody. His earliest memories included his mother asking him repeatedly if he was *in one of his black moods again*. Maroon had never figured out if his moods were situational, chemical, psychological, or spiritual. It didn't seem to matter. All he could do was endure them while trying not to let them tear the fabric of the relationships that supported him and through which he supported others.

Maroon made no effort early on this morning to diagnose the cause or contributing factors for his inner darkness. Robinson's previous day's counsel had seemed to discourage doing so. More disgusted with himself for his black mood than feeling entitled to it, Maroon resolved to get some exercise in the early morning dawn. Exercise often cleared away the tangle of darkness.

Maroon made his way out the back of his residence, through the rolling cemetery, and toward the lakefront a half mile to the west. Reaching the lakefront overlook, Maroon decided to continue on down to the beach and, if he felt up to it, out to the end of the pier. He hadn't walked to the pier's end in some time. The water was unusually still, almost glass-like. He could imagine that its peaceful lapping against the pier might somehow settle his inner stewing.

As Maroon reached the pier, he found it empty, not unusual for early morning, other than when salmon were running up the river, when one might expect to see several people fishing. A light early morning mist hovered over the water around the pier. He resolved to stroll to the pier's end, circle the lighthouse, and return home.

Maroon usually enjoyed the walk out on the pier, farther out on the lake than anyone had a right to expect. Following the dire warnings on the signs prominently displayed at the pier's beginning, Maroon was always cautious to assess the safety of venturing out on the pier. Lake swells breaking over the pier head could be large. Waves sweeping the length of the pier could wash off even the strongest and most intrepid adventurer. But not on this day, with the water like glass.

Within a couple of minutes, Maroon had reached the lighthouse at the pier's end. He sometimes just tapped the lighthouse wall and turned back. But with the waters so still this morning, he resolved to continue on around the lighthouse to circle back. The view off the very end of the pier might be especially encouraging.

No sooner had Maroon rounded the lighthouse than he noticed a female figure standing at the pier's edge, gazing out across the still waters. Maroon immediately thought of his encounter with Robinson the day before. He hadn't expected to see anyone. But here was a lone figure, dressed much as Robinson had dressed, appearing transfixed with the vision of the early morning sun streaming through the light mist hovering over the still waters.

Maroon stopped, himself transfixed at the sight of the regal woman, whose visage he could only partly make out as she stared out across the waters. Maroon wasn't sure later how long the moment had lasted, the two figures frozen in time and place. But eventually, the woman's quiet words, uttered without moving or turning to address Maroon, freed him from his transfixion.

"The moment captured us, didn't it?" she asked.

Maroon nodded, foolishly, given that the woman hadn't turned to see his reaction. But still staring out across the water, the woman seemed to know.

"He said you'd understand," she continued.

Her comment confirmed for Maroon that he had met River Woman, Robinson's wife. He didn't even need to ask. Waiting patiently for her next words, Maroon turned his gaze from the woman to the still waters beyond, the mist above now lit brilliantly by the low rays of the early morning sun.

In his brief research into Robinson's life the day before, Maroon had learned a few spare bits about River Woman. Unlike Robinson and his first wife Flying Cloud, River Woman and Robinson had no children. But they had lived long and engaging lives together.

River Woman learned the English language as a child in Reverend Ferry's mission school on Mackinac Island. Many years later, the Baptist minister Reverend Leon Slater married River Woman to Robinson at Slater's mission located in present-day Grand Rapids, where Slater cared for 150 Native American families. Once married to Robinson, River Woman had helped Robinson run his string of up to twenty outposts along the Grand River, of which the as-yet-unnamed Grand Haven at the river's mouth was her favorite. It had a store, warehouse, and dwelling house with four rooms.

Robinson's inland trading post at the confluence of the Grand River and its Thornapple River tributary, at present-day Ada, was River Woman's next favorite. While Robinson had built the Grand Haven post, he had acquired the upriver post from the half-French and half-Indian Madame LaFramboise, whose trader husband, an Indian had murdered at the post. Madame LaFramboise had continued to trade at the post in the winters, taking her furs north to Mackinac Island in the summers, where she built a fine home with her considerable profits.

Robinson had been glad to acquire Madame LaFramboise's trading post, for the profits, influence, and access it gave Robinson. The emerging Grand Rapids area would soon become Robinson's seat of commercial success and political office and influence. River Woman, coming from a tribal chieftain line, had been glad for her own position of influence among the area's tribes. Grand Rapids was their power base, while Grand Haven was their lakeshore retreat, much as Grand Haven is for influential Grand Rapidians today. Some things change. Others don't.

As much as River Woman loved Robinson and appreciated his strict devotion as a husband, River woman's greatest interest was in Indian affairs, not in trading or land settlement. She was proud of her Indian heritage and not generally willing to engage with lesser others, knowing English well but preferring only to speak the several Indian dialects she knew. In both cases, her preferred company and language, though, she made an exception for Maroon.

"It's sacred, isn't it?" River Woman asked Maroon without averting her gaze from the brilliantly lit mist hanging over the still waters.

Maroon still stood silently behind her, slightly to her side from where he could just make out her noble demeanor and fixed vision.

"Tell me more," Maroon heard himself answer without otherwise stirring, other than to nod in agreement, although once again he doubted that River Woman would see him where he stood.

They were the first words Maroon had spoken. He already knew that River Woman would speak with him only sparingly, indeed if he were not careful, then only condescendingly. He wanted to say nothing more than necessary to permit her to impart whatever wisdom or message she, Robinson, or Ferry wished to convey. He didn't want to break the early morning's spell, transfixing their encounter.

"It's all given over to the highest being," River Woman said, this time tipping her head slightly to shake it gently back and forth as she spoke, almost as if she were teaching or correcting a small child. She added, "Just as we must live."

Maroon let River Woman's spare words sink deep into his soul. Yet he felt that she had invited another inquiry, without which she might not speak.

"Is that how Robinson lived?" Maroon heard himself asking, although instantly regretting his question, which seemed more prying or even challenging than respectful and wisdom seeking, which is what Maroon had intended. Maroon watched the noble woman carefully for sign of her reaction, hoping that she would continue without offense. After what Maroon took to be the slightest huff of regret for the universally fallen and imperfect human condition, River Woman answered.

"More so than most," she said, pausing only briefly before adding humbly, "More so than me. It was a time of great change."

The two stared out across the still waters again, long enough for a deep breath or two of peace in which the echoes of River Woman's words subsided. She then resumed, saying only, "And you?"

Maroon, though, had lost his train of thought, mesmerized by the brilliant mist and solemn exchange. In a near panic for not wanting their conversation to end, Maroon grasped for what the noble woman was asking.

Sensing Maroon's struggle behind her, River Woman turned slowly to face Maroon. For the first time, their eyes met. And in that moment, Maroon's knees nearly buckled under him. It took every bit of resolve he had just to stand, respectfully facing the implacably regal woman. Fortunately, River Woman spoke, this time without reserve.

"Are you living in the sacred intersection of time and space?"

It was Maroon's turn to huff in regret for the universally fallen and imperfect human condition. He nonetheless felt the urge to answer as respectfully as he could.

"Not so much as you or Robinson," Maroon breathed as simply and humbly as he could.

To Maroon's surprise, River Woman smiled. To that point, her implacable, regal, almost stern visage had given no hint that she was capable of sharing any joy, no less any companionable conversation. Maroon, though, had apparently found just the right note.

"I hope you'll remember our time and conversation," River Woman said gently through her smile, adding, "We'd better be going."

Indeed, Maroon could sense activity behind him along the pier, presumably of footfalls and fishing casts from early morning anglers. He stole a glance over his shoulder, but the lighthouse blocked his vision. Turning back with his mouth open to speak, Maroon saw that she had gone, vanished like vapor in the brilliant mist.

Maroon dropped slowly to his knees on the pier's ruddy concrete, not in confusion or wonder, as one might expect, but in overwhelming acknowledgment of the sacred. The earth's intersection with the higher realm, from which its creator governed it, had opened. Maroon could not stand on its hallowed ground. He bowed his head, hearing only his own breath, moving in unison with the slightest sound of the rise and fall of the waters along the pier's edge.

When he rose again, Maroon could tell, from the higher angle of the sun streaming across the waters surrounding the pier, that some time had passed. He was still alone on the small platform at the pier's end. When he rounded the lighthouse to head back down the pier to shore, he saw a handful of individuals fishing or strolling. One of them was taking photographs in the brilliant morning sun, as it dissipated the faint remaining mist.

As Maroon began his hike back, he felt an exhilaration he hadn't felt in a very long time. His black mood of the early morning had disappeared like the morning mist. His pace quickened until he began to run, not hurriedly but lightly, joyfully, out of an excess of exuberance. He hadn't run in a very long time.

4

Oddly, Maroon didn't think much throughout the rest of the day about his encounter with River Woman. Her visit seemed to have knit his encounters with Ferry and Robinson together into a sensible whole. Maroon's only significant reflection that day was that perhaps, now that he had a neat little troika of visits, the encounters were done.

Maroon sensed that he was ready for the visits to end. They were plainly priceless, worth their weight in gold. He wouldn't have given them up for anything, except perhaps for the peace he had long sought, when that seemed to be their purpose, to bring him peace. But the visits were also taxing, mentally and emotionally. He even laughed quietly to himself that if he had one or two more visits, he might just not make it. It might all be too much.

And so Maroon went through his day deliberately taking no account of his encounter with River Woman. After all, hadn't that been Robinson's counsel, to take less account while instead living more? By day's end, Maroon was simply exhausted, more tired than usual, drained, he assumed, in large part by the morning's exquisite encounter. He went to bed with a silent prayer that he have no more.

Maroon fell instantly asleep, which was not unusual. His wife would typically lay awake, even for hours on end, processing her day or planning the next, before finally falling asleep after midnight. Maroon was instead typically out cold within minutes, mentally exhausted. And this night, he was more exhausted than most.

Yet just after midnight, Maroon snapped back awake. He wasn't sure what had awoken him. The dogs may have stirred, or maybe his wife had just finally fallen asleep, appointing him sentinel to the night. Whatever was the cause, he was awake, fully awake.

Maroon remained awake for the rest of the night, tossing and turning. For the first hour, he lay quietly, not minding having a spell to reflect. But soon, his light ruminations accelerated until he was talking to himself, animatedly, on random subjects. He could even tell that his thoughts were neither processing the prior day nor preparing for the next. They were just frivolous repetitions and speculations, adorned by his intensifying inner speech.

Maroon at first tried his usual tricks to return to restful retirement. He recited the Orthodox Jesus Prayer, repeatedly, examining and paraphrasing each of its four brief phrases. No luck. Wide awake. He then recalled the evening's baseball score and the record with which it left his team, projecting it out to season's end to assess the final record. Still no luck. Wide awake. He planned his morning's exercise. Still no luck. He remained wide awake.

Maroon rolled out of bed at his usual time, only having cat-napped for the last hour or so. He rose just as exhausted as he had retired the evening before. Whatever exuberance his River Woman encounter had generated was gone.

No early morning walks or rides today, Maroon resolved. He didn't expect another other-worldly encounter, nor did he desire one. And so he wasn't going to entice one. He needed recovery time. He'd stick to the house and work that morning.

As the day wore on and the long night receded into the past, though, Maroon recovered a little of his energy. By early afternoon, he was ready for a break from writing at home, even if only a short break. He decided to take a short walk through Duncan Woods.

Duncan Memorial Park, or *Duncan Woods* as locals know it, is an extraordinary forty acres of old-growth hemlock, beech, oak, and maple forest roughly in the middle of Grand Haven. The lumber industry stripped Michigan of its forests in the latter half of the 1800s. The Old-Growth Forest Network, the only national registry of old-growth woods, lists Duncan Woods among fewer than a dozen Michigan old-growth sites.

Grand Haven

About 150 years have passed since lumbermen felled Michigan's forests to rebuild Chicago after its great 1871 fire and to build new settlements across Michigan and throughout the Midwest. But the regenerated woods and forests still lack the old-growth character of a never-cut glen. Maroon considered it an extraordinary blessing to live alongside Duncan Woods, the western border of which touches the city's great cemetery.

Maroon had walked Duncan Woods so often and for so many years that he had no particular path through or around it. He tended to just wander this way and that. As a city park, Duncan Woods hosted quite a few walkers. Beaten trails went this way and that way. But the advisory board directing the park's management had intentionally left the trails mostly undeveloped. Duncan Woods has a single asphalt drive cutting through its center, half of it blocked off from cars for only pedestrian use. Otherwise, one wandered up and down its forested hills at will, largely unguided.

Maroon had intended only a short circuit. But as he made his way deeper into the woods, his wandering took him up a path along a ridge, snaking between small hemlocks, toward the highest point in the woods. He hadn't been up to that spot in years. While he liked the ridge hike, he sometimes found teenagers lounging in hammocks there, smoking marijuana or doing other things teenagers do in out-of-the-way places. He had abandoned the site for that reason or simply because of the increasing effort the hill hike took, harder in Maroon's advancing age.

This day, though, no teenagers hid among the smaller trees atop the hill. Maroon did notice a spry older female figure, though. Maroon thought of turning back to avoid her. He didn't want to startle or concern anyone. Just as he prepared to turn, though, the figure caught sight of Maroon and smiled.

The figure's smile trapped Maroon. He would seem furtive to spin on the spot, just short of the hill's crest, to avoid the figure. Better, Maroon reasoned, to walk on politely past the smiling figure and down the hill's other side, as he had intended.

Maroon nodded a return smile at the figure as he approached but then politely looked down at the path, beginning to take a respectfully wide swath around her so as not to alarm her with his proximity.

"Maroon!" the slight elderly woman called to him, slowing his last uphill trek to the hilltop where she stood.

He looked up at the smiling woman, trying to recognize her face. The cemetery and Duncan Woods brought these reacquaintances with some regularity. Maroon had met all kinds of townsfolk in the woods or cemetery over the years, many whom he hadn't known frequented the place. Lately, in his advancing years, the encounters had grown fewer, his steady commerce among the local population having waned. He had fewer acquaintances.

Maroon was also finding it harder to recognize the acquaintances he encountered. Age had its deceptive effect on appearances. The passage of time had its equally deceptive effect on memory. Maroon did not recognize the woman, despite her recognizing him.

"Good to see you!" Maroon returned the woman's greeting with a broadening smile, while hoping that he had expressed sufficient warmth. He kept moving, although more slowly, trying to judge whether she wished him to stop and chat.

"Are you enjoying my woods?" the woman asked just as Maroon reached her.

Maroon took the inquiry as a signal that he was to stop. He did so, respectfully nodding in answer. He was enjoying the woods. At the same time, though, Maroon wondered at the woman's reference to *my woods*. She had given him a hint of her identity but one that he could not at all make out.

"I'm so glad," the woman resumed, acknowledging Maroon's nod. She added, "My husband and I intended for you to enjoy it. You know, he was a lawyer like you."

Maroon searched frantically through his lawyer acquaintances, including those recently departed, trying to piece together the woman's hints of identity. But Maroon remained at a loss.

Yet then it struck him. He had been searching the wrong frame of reference. He was not greeting an old friend. He had instead stumbled upon his next otherworldly encounter. The woman before him was, with her lawyer husband, the donor of Duncan Woods.

Maroon knew little of the couple's donation of the woods, only that it had occurred quite a while ago. He knew only that the city held the woods in trust for preservation of its old-growth forest and use as an unspoiled and undeveloped park. A lawyer friend of Maroon's had been on the woods' advisory board years ago. He had explained to Maroon the donors' intentions not to change the woods or even to develop it as a park, although its heavy use had forced the board to spread bark over some of its many trails to reduce hillside erosion.

Whatever the advisory board's concerns and methods, they had worked. The woods, with enormous living trees, large standing dead woods, and huge twisted deadfalls, were a spectacular throwback to another time. Despite the park's relatively heavy use, the woods also hosted deer, fox, owls, pileated woodpeckers, and other shy wild residents.

"You and your husband had great foresight," Maroon replied with an appreciative nod and smile, picking up on Mrs. Duncan's hints.

Maroon breathed a silent sigh of relief, having navigated the encounter's uncertain introduction. Where would it lead, though? He searched his memory for any other details about the woods and their donation, while he waited for Mrs. Duncan's reply.

"Oh, he was the one with the foresight," Mrs. Duncan replied wistfully. After a moment's pause, she continued, "Maybe it was his legal training or just because he loved the woods so much. The two certainly came together in the gift of this place."

Maroon would confirm with some light research that evening that Martha Duncan had gifted the forty acres to the city in 1913, a half century or more after her husband had acquired it. Robert Duncan had visited Grand Haven in 1851, falling in love with the place. He soon moved his law practice to the second floor of a downtown drug store, as settlers, lumbermen, and land speculators began flooding the still-pristine region. Duncan was one of the first two lawyers to permanently move their practices to Grand Haven.

Robert Duncan, like the lumbermen and land speculators he joined in Grand Haven, kept a sharp eye out for business opportunities. His thriving law practice enabled him to purchase hundreds of acres of land surrounding the settlement. Some of it went for lumbering and to sell off in small parcels to settlers. But when the forty acres of untouched woods became available just outside the city's early boundaries, Duncan had another idea for it.

Duncan built a grand home at the edge of the woods, right at the bend in Lake Avenue. The home overlooked what would become Duncan Woods. Martha Duncan, twenty-one years younger than Robert, joined him in that home, writing later of how she loved looking at the woods through the home's kitchen window as she washed dishes.

Duncan didn't initially share the woods with the townsfolk. Indeed, he earned a grouch's reputation for chasing children and others from the woods, which he hoped to retain in pristine state as lumbermen cut the surrounding forests. Duncan mostly succeeded, both in preserving the woods and keeping it relatively pristine, until the city surrounded it. After Duncan's demise, Martha gifted it to the city's people with a trust to maintain it and a restriction to keep it as natural as possible. A half century of use exhausted the trust, but others donated additional funds and services, and the city took on the rest. The park remains a gift from the past and a promise for the future.

Maroon let Mrs. Duncan's words, crediting her husband's vision for the gift, soak into the surrounding hilltop greenery. The trees atop the hill were smaller, some of them bent and twisted by the winds. The magnificent old-growth trees stood deep in the glens, with their surrounding dunes protecting them from the winds. Maroon's willingness to wait and listen, a skill his interrogations as a lawyer had honed, paid off. Mrs. Duncan soon resumed.

"He always said that one cannot truly live in the present," Mrs. Duncan reflected, again with a far-off look. When she stole a glance at Maroon for his reaction, Maroon tipped his head in respectful interest. Mrs. Duncan took his encouragement to continue.

"He'd say that the past is gone and the present evanescent," Mrs. Duncan ventured hesitantly, before continuing, "We must live in the future because only the future welcomes our purpose, and purpose is the only way in which we draw meaning from the world."

Mrs. Duncan paused for a brief giggle, before adding with a sheepish bob of her head, as if she had spoken beyond her capability, "I think that's how he'd put it."

To Maroon, though, Mrs. Duncan looked quite capable, even comfortable, with such thoughts, even though they were fresh, surprising, and pleasing to him. Maroon instantly knew that Mrs. Duncan had just given him another gift of insight, likely the one her otherworldly appearance intended to deliver. At the same time, Maroon appreciated Mrs. Duncan's humility and sensibility, which Maroon rightly suspected Mrs. Duncan had used well throughout her many years of living with a prominent lawyer with clear and firm intentions, more-than-capable articulation, and a reputation for grousing at children.

"How does one live with such foresight?" Maroon heard himself ask, glad that his intuition had generated an inquiry to continue the conversation.

Yet Mrs. Duncan only laughed, replying, "You'd have to ask him. But I suspect you already know. And if you don't know, I suspect you could construe your answer from what I just shared of what my husband said. You lawyers have ways of figuring things out."

Mrs. Duncan laughed again at her lawyer jest. Maroon, though, felt the sting of Mrs. Duncan's light rebuke, recognizing at the same time that she was entirely within her rights to share it. Maroon had asked for more, when Mrs. Duncan had already delivered two gifts, one of the great old-forest park and the other of her husband's wisdom.

But Mrs. Duncan didn't want Maroon to linger with any sting.

"Look," Mrs. Duncan said excitedly while pointing in the direction of a shadow that had just seemed to swoop through the trees toward the bottom of one of the surrounding glens. She added, "That's my dear owl. I'm afraid we've disturbed him."

Maroon followed Mrs. Duncan's gaze and outstretched arm, searching for sight of the owl but unable to make out its disappearing flight. When he turned back to Mrs. Duncan, she was gone, disappearing in flight like her dear owl.

Maroon smiled. He had expected her otherworldly disappearance, so like the ones the days before. This time, no emotion, insight, or other sensation overwhelmed him. Maroon simply shook his head while wearing a wry smile. He was adjusting well to his enchanted world. And he appreciated its accumulating insights.

5

With Mrs. Duncan gone and her insight imparted, Maroon had nothing to do other than to return home from the Duncan Woods hilltop, about a ten to fifteen-minute pleasant downhill stroll in all. As he descended the hill, one careful step at a time over the many tree roots that erosion had exposed in the steep trail, he reflected on Mrs. Duncan's insight, or rather, the insight with which she credited her lawyer husband.

The past is gone and present evanescent, Maroon rehearsed. Wasn't that what she had said?

Maroon knew from his law studies, practice, and teaching that if he didn't soon rehearse what he had heard, he might well forever forget it. He had learned, for instance, to immediately repeat a name when newly introduced and to repeat the name again on departure. Doing so helped to move the new name, so easy to immediately forget, from short-term to long-term memory. Otherwise, Maroon was as bad at names as anyone else.

Maroon also knew that elaborating what he had just learned, whether paraphrasing, extending, or analyzing it, would further aid in memory. And so, he turned Mrs. Duncan's, or *Mr.* Duncan's, phrase over in his mind.

Surely, the past is indeed gone, Maroon considered, although he felt that to forget the past can be to repeat it. Agreed, he didn't want to live in the past. Indeed, he could only do so figuratively, not literally, given the past's definition, while living in the past even figuratively can be highly problematic. He wouldn't forget the past, but he also wouldn't live in the past, blind to the new opportunities and challenges of the present.

Yet the idea that one can also not live *in the present* was certainly counterintuitive, Maroon reasoned. The popular mantra was exactly the opposite. Didn't nearly every self-help guru urge *living in the moment*? What had Mr. Duncan discovered?

As Maroon reached the bottom of the hill and turned toward home, he remembered that Mrs. Duncan had given a further clue to the insight. What had she said? Maroon wracked his brain to recall her words. Something about living in the future because *the future holds our purpose*. Yes, that was it. Maroon could just hear the echo of Mrs.

Duncan's giggle, just after having added something about purpose being *the way we draw meaning from the world*.

Maroon turned the last phrases over and over in his mind, so intensely that his wandering took him a wider way home, not through the cemetery's edge but along an opposite ridge to the east, overlooking an elementary school playground.

In his reflection, Maroon guessed that Mr. Duncan was right as to the first part. Only the future can hold our purpose because purpose projects forward to possibilities and potential, not backward to the completed past. But what should Maroon make of the corollary insight that purpose is how we draw meaning from the world?

Maroon was aware of the criticism that moderns, or more accurately *post-modernists*, wrongly treat the world as a set of projections. They conceive that the world is simply material without meaning and that their own mind is the only thing giving it meaning. Yet Maroon had learned that the world is laden with meaning. The human mind doesn't so much project meaning as receive it. Like it or not, things speak their meaning to the observer, even inanimate things like a stump inviting one to sit or a cup inviting one to sip.

And therein lay the revelation Maroon sought, presumably one that Mr. and Mrs. Duncan had intended in delivering the message. We grasp things, literally and figuratively, only by their meaning. One lifts a cup to drink, for drinking is a cup's first purpose. One sits on a chair, for sitting is what makes a chair more than a pile of sticks or a stump.

Pausing at the ridge's overlook of the elementary school playground, Maroon tried to extend the insight into a broader application. What was *his* purpose in life, with the things for which he grasped and the places where he sat? How did *his* purpose draw meaning from the world and possibilities from the future?

A joyful noise, though, distracted Maroon's reflection. Standing on the ridge overlooking the playground, Maroon realized that schoolchildren were running gleefully about the grassy field below him, enjoying a recess. Maroon smiled, soaking up the joy the children's happy shrieks, shouts, and chatter transmitted.

But wait, Maroon suddenly thought. It was summer. School was out. Maroon had many times enjoyed the hidden view of the schoolchildren playing on the elementary school field below the tree-covered Duncan Woods ridge. Yet he should not be enjoying such a view now, with school out for the summer.

"It's beautiful, isn't it?" a female voice breathed into Maroon's ear from just behind.

Maroon would have jumped, had it not been for his several encounters in the past couple of days. But strangely, the voice hadn't startled Maroon. He had nearly expected it, given the incongruence of his vision of the schoolchildren at play below, in high summer.

Maroon didn't even turn to acknowledge the female figure, standing just behind him and to his right, where his peripheral vision could just make her out. He instead simply kept watching the children at play, nodding slowly while waiting for the female figure to continue. Maroon even chuckled silently to himself for already having a hint of who the figure might be. He was getting pretty good at this game of otherworldly encounters, he figured.

"Nothing lifts my spirit more than hearing the children at play," the woman behind Maroon breathed into his ear.

Maroon nodded again. This time, though, he turned to acknowledge the woman, not wanting to appear disrespectful.

"So good to make your acquaintance, Miss White," Maroon greeted her, intuitively adopting what he imagined might have been the tone of a mid-1800s greeting between older strangers of the opposite sex.

"And good to make yours, Maroon," the matronly figure replied with a nod, accompanied by the slightest indication of a curtsy.

The elementary school over which Maroon and Mary A. White looked from the Duncan Woods ridge bore the schoolteacher's name, given in her honor when the school opened in 1959. Miss White, though, had come to Grand Haven more than a century earlier, in the summer of 1835, to join her sister Amanda White Ferry, the wife of the town's founder Reverend William Ferry. Miss White's memorial stood among the other town founder memorials on the nearby cemetery overlook where Maroon had met Ferry just days before.

Mary White joined her sister and brother-in-law in Grand Haven to teach school, becoming the first schoolteacher not only in the town but in the region. Maroon knew a little of Miss White's history, more than the history of some of the other town founders. Maroon's wife and daughter had each attended Mary A. White Elementary, which lay just over a dune ridge from Maroon's own residence.

Although she taught school in the remotest of outposts, Mary White came from royal schoolteacher lineage. She had studied back home in Massachusetts at the Buckland School under Mary Lyon, founder of Mount Holyoke College for Women.

Miss White had no children of her own. She was betrothed to a physician who died just a week before their planned marriage ceremony. Fatefully, her schoolchildren would instead be her adopted brood. Mary White's first Grand Haven students, taught in the attic of her sister's home, included her sister's three boys plus two boys and a girl, children of the French-Canadian fur trader Pierre Duvernay and his Native American wife. Three sons of Timothy Eastman, a medical doctor moving to Grand Haven from Maine, soon joined them, giving Miss White a challenging class of eight frontier boys and one girl.

To make her teaching challenges even greater, Miss White taught adult trappers, traders, sailors, and lumberjacks evening classes. The sailors spread word around the Great Lakes of her skill, bringing her more short-term adult evening students. Within a year, classes had moved from Ferry's attic to a new school building in town that also served as a church on Sunday and courthouse as needed. Miss White taught Sunday school classes on the Lord's day and sewing and handiwork classes to girls on Saturday, giving her a seven-day-a-week vocation.

Mary White labored on in Grand Haven for a decade and a half before moving to Illinois in 1851 to teach and serve as accountant at a female college seminary. Yet after a decade of serving higher education, Miss White returned to her beloved Grand Haven to resume her local teaching duties.

And when she could no longer teach in her later years, she kept house for one of her first students, Reverend Ferry's bachelor son Thomas White Ferry, who by then had become a U.S. senator.

Miss White's indomitable presence would continue to grace the community into the next century. She did not pass on until the summer of 1901.

Standing on the ridge like a cowed schoolchild in front of her, Maroon regarded the indefatigable Miss White, dressed formally in the manner Maroon imagined she would have taught. Realizing that she expected him to speak, Maroon ventured, with a warm smile of appreciation for the gay playground activity behind him, "A joyful noise indeed, although I wouldn't wish to be a child again."

Miss White smiled back at Maroon but gently shook her head, replying with a schoolteacher's deft touch of correction, "Now, Maroon, you know better than that. Haven't you done your reading?"

Maroon raised his eyebrows in surprise. But at the same moment, he realized that he should have known better. These figures visiting him didn't come to receive and share Maroon's insights. They instead came to impart their own wisdom or the messages assigned them to share.

Maroon swiftly adjusted his frame, replying kindly to Miss White, "Please forgive me. What did my reading overlook?"

Miss White smiled appreciatively at the humility of Maroon's reply. She hadn't expected a battle of wits from Maroon, as she would have expected from one of her frontier schoolboys. But she was glad nonetheless to avoid it.

"We are to retain the heart of a child, ready to welcome our Father's embrace, aren't we?" Miss White inquired of Maroon, once again as if leading a wayward student through forgotten but familiar paces.

"Indeed, we are," Maroon replied with a pained smile of regret, offered in remission of his waywardness. Yet Maroon wasn't an entirely docile student. He continued, "But what does it mean to display the heart of a child?"

"Oh, my friend, let us not tempt the Lord with our foolishness," the matron replied, adding, "You know that he desires nothing greater from us than our steady devotion, just as a child must respect and obey the child's earthly father."

"Am I to become a child again, then?" Maroon replied, this time more to tease the matron and to play along.

Miss White would have admonished Maroon again if she had not instantly perceived his playfulness. So instead, she suggested only, "We must remember and recover who we were as children, not in immaturity or rebellious spirit but in innocence."

"So innocent of the world though wise of its ways?" Maroon suggested back to Miss White.

"Now you have it," the matron affirmed with a warm smile.

The happy squeals and shouts of the schoolchildren in the field below rang up again over the ridge on which Maroon and Miss White stood. Maroon thought for a moment that their encounter might have reached its end. But he instead sensed that the matron had not yet imparted the message the encounter intended. So Maroon ventured again, "Might I ask what we mean by *innocence*?"

This time, Miss White gave a far-off look above the field below them, to the horizon beyond, where the next dune, this one covered with streets and residences, rose. After a decent pause, Miss White shifted her gaze back to Maroon.

"To answer your question directly," she began, "Innocence means not to participate in what we know is not our purpose or end. Participation belies purpose. Participate only in that which is your end."

Maroon understood exactly what Miss White intended. Yet he also read in her reply and tone a willingness to say somewhat more. And so he made one last try to elicit the full flower of her message.

"And if that is your direct answer, which I fully understand and deeply appreciate," Maroon began, "Then what would be your indirect answer to my query?"

"I know this construct lies outside the culture of your day, much as it wasn't entirely within the culture of my own day," Miss White replied, "But we participate in the divine liturgy. Discover the broadest form of that liturgy and deepest meaning of divinity, and you will have lived your purpose, dear Maroon."

Maroon nodded, taking a deep breath as he did so. He knew it was time for him to turn his gaze from Miss White to the field below, so that Miss White could take her leave discreetly. He knew that when he turned back, she would be gone through the wilds of the woods, like Mrs. Duncan and her dear owl. Maroon didn't want Miss White to go. He had felt a warmth and matronly love from her the other figures, even the kindly Mrs. Duncan, had not conveyed. But he knew that to turn to the field, he must, to let Miss White go.

To Maroon's surprise, when he turned to watch the schoolchildren on the field below, they were gone. Not surprisingly, Miss White was gone when Maroon turned back.

Maroon stood on the ridge, looking out across the empty field, rehearsing what Miss White had said so that he would not forget. He then made his way slowly back home, compelled to consider in another light the inexplicable recent events. Heretofore, he had experienced only one otherworldly encounter per day, giving him the rest of the day, evening, and night to digest events. Now, though, his short afternoon walk had brought not one but two strange encounters. Whatever entity or phenomenon was arranging or triggering the encounters was accelerating the pace.

Moreover, Maroon's previous encounters had involved only the sudden appearance and disappearance of a single historical figure. This most-recent event, though, had involved the appearance and disappearance of both a historical figure and a full field of schoolchildren. Whatever entity or phenomenon was arranging or triggering the encounters was broadening their cosmic reach.

Once home, Maroon resolved to take a step back for a broader view of what might be going on, as soon as he found the time. Perhaps he'd even have a chat with his wife, which to this point he had resisted. For the rest of the day, though, he had matters to which to attend.

6

That evening, Maroon found an occasion to inquire of his wife whether she saw any signs in Maroon of mental decline or delusion. In posing the question, he tried not to suggest that he saw any signs himself. He instead wanted her neutral opinion.

Maroon's intuition that his wife would try to see through the seeming innocence of his question for the root of his concern was correct. She plied Maroon with questions, which Maroon did his best to fend off. He wasn't ready to admit that he just experienced several days of extraordinary encounters with historical figures. She would rightly have judged him mad and demanded a psychiatric examination. Maroon, though, wasn't up to either the condemnation or the examination.

In the end, Maroon learned that his wife had detected nothing unusual, which isn't to say that Maroon was a usual sort of fellow. He wasn't usual at all, although no one truly is. The most ordinary-looking folk are usually the least ordinary, simply better at disguising their rank peculiarities. Maroon's peculiarities, though, had remained consistent recently, in his wife's well-informed view.

Maroon wrung from his wife the concession that she would alert him if she saw anything out of character in his mental acuity or disposition. His usual oddities, she would ignore, as she had learned to do over the course of their several-decades-long marriage.

For his part, Maroon agreed to alert his wife if he saw anything peculiar in her own presentation or disposition, although they both knew that his assurances were false. He would do nothing of the sort. By bearing his child, keeping their house, and forgiving his many offenses, she had earned his consent to be as eccentric as she pleased, without Maroon calling her on it.

Maroon, though, had greater concern that his mental health might be declining as a course of disease, rather than merely aging, than any concern his wife had. His wife's parents had both lived into their nineties without any drastic decline in their cognition. She presumably had the same hardy genes.

Maroon's parents, by contrast, had passed in their seventies, each after having exhibited such crippling mental and related physical declines as to need institutional care, a heritage reflected in their own parents' early demise.

Moreover, Maroon's mother had died of dementia. She had imagined all sorts of incredible happenings before her institutionalization. She had lost all sense of person, time, and place after her institutionalization. Although Maroon took reasonable care of his health, he imagined that he might well meet a similar demise. He even considered that his mother's dementia was already upon him.

Yet Maroon seemed, from his wife's testimony and his own evaluation, to be doing fine, or at least no less well than usual, but for the otherworldly encounters of the very-recent days. And those encounters hadn't unhinged him unduly. He had instead been able to keep them confidential. He would watch for evidence of decline. So would his wife. But for now, he remained in the clear, except for what to do about the increasing visitations.

Maroon spent his few free moments throughout the late afternoon and evening recalling and considering Miss White's urging to *participate in the divine liturgy*. Maroon knew that she didn't necessarily mean to regularly attend a certain church service of specific liturgical form. Rather, Maroon inferred that Miss White was referring to the cosmic structure, its hierarchy, and its cadence, in all that humans say, see, and do.

Formal worship might well promote one's participation in the divine liturgy, but an occasional or even regular Sunday worship wouldn't alone be enough. For a full participation, wringing everything out of life it offered, one must instead shape one's daily and moment-by-moment activities to the divine order and divinity's desires. Such was the divine liturgy's broader form and deeper meaning.

Maroon ended the day as he had ended the several prior days, mentally and emotionally exhausted. Unfortunately, he dreamed raging nightmares once again for much of the night. He awoke with barely more mental energy than he had ended the prior day, too little mental energy to even think of continuing with his assigned writing. The writing would have to wait another day. He was far ahead of schedule with it in any case, as was his habit.

Maroon's wife, though, had other plans for Maroon than the rest he sought, felt he deserved, and felt even more that he badly needed.

One of Maroon's few other contributions to the welfare of his own family, beyond the law practice, teaching, and writing with which he earned the family's income, was to make wood furniture to his wife's specifications, whatever she felt was the family's need.

The furniture and furnishing projects had been many over the years. Maroon had made kitchen cabinets, stand-alone cupboards, living-room built-in cabinetry, office desks, dining tables, side tables, coffee tables, and shelves. He had made wood boxes, bookends, display trays, cutting boards, coasters, and picture frames. If wood was the material and home furnishing the need, Maroon was for hire, and inexpensively. Maroon's wife would tease him that she would pay him well, even if payment would come out of his own paycheck deposited directly to their marital account that Maroon's wife alone controlled.

Maroon didn't mind the wood projects. The spatial reckoning they required was a pleasant break from the textual reasoning with which Maroon constantly dealt, in his law practice and teaching and his legal writing. Maroon's reward, though, came with his wife's oohs and aahs over the finished project or, when she wasn't that impressed, with her general satisfaction.

And so when Maroon arose to the happy chatter of his genial wife, he learned his day's assignment. His day would begin at the local lumber yard, not the town's big-box home-improvement outlet but the actual old lumber yard, hard by the railroad tracks that once delivered its material.

The lumbering history of Grand Haven is quite an extraordinary tale, even if a relatively brief one. The lumber industry in West Michigan seemed perfectly designed to serve the building needs of the exploding settler population of the Upper Midwest from about 1840 to 1890. Michigan's Lower Peninsula was a vast uncut, old-growth forest.

The Grand River, emptying into Lake Michigan precisely at Grand Haven, and its several major navigable tributaries, covered a vast portion of the Lower Peninsula, in some places well more than two-thirds of the way across the whole state. Those waterways were the perfect delivery route to float lumber down to Grand Haven for milling, to load onto boats plying the whole of the Great Lakes and its other river waterways, distributing the milled lumber.

Within the span of about fifty years, lumbermen had logged out most of the state. Lumbermen moved their operations north into Canada and west to other forested regions. But those lumbermen left behind well-built settlements and extraordinary wealth that fueled the mercantile businesses, manufacturing, tourism, and other industries that replaced lumbering for local occupation and profit.

Maroon parked his pickup truck alongside the lumber yard's large, old wooden structure with a railway spur, no longer in use, running down the interior center of it. Inside the structure stood piles of sweet-smelling pine, poplar, maple, oak, and other hardwoods, cut to all convenient sizes or milled into intricate trim patterns.

With the hour still early, Maroon stood in the long structure's door, taking in the lumber's special sight and smell, anticipating the pleasure of getting to work that day with a small piece of it. Maroon even thought that keeping himself busy indoors that day with his wife's wood project would forestall any further otherworldly encounters, at least for a day.

"Smell that wood, eh?" a voice intoned from behind Maroon.

Maroon turned to see a smaller, elderly figure, one who might, by build and dress, have been a banker or merchant at a younger age. The figure had indeed been both, among other things, including above all a lumberman.

Maroon opened his mouth to reply but found no words. The fact that he didn't recognize the figure as a friend or acquaintance had already supplied the only clue Maroon needed that he had met his next otherworldly figure. But who was the historical figure? Fortunately, the man extended his right hand, which Maroon took with his own right hand to accept a firm handshake.

"Dwight Cutler," the elderly gentleman introduced himself, adding, "Glad to meet you, Maroon."

Maroon didn't immediately recognize the name. Its vaguely familiar sound made Maroon pause to wonder if his law practice might have brought him into the elderly figure's orbit at some distant point in the past. But no, Cutler had used Maroon's name, while simultaneously acknowledging that this moment was their first meeting. Surely, Cutler was from a much earlier day, far enough back to make his appearance Maroon's next celestial encounter.

And then it hit Maroon: the smell of the wood. Cutler shared with Maroon, Maroon's own love for the smell of wood, especially pine wood and other timber with aromatic resins.

Maroon knew that Cutler was a historic name in Grand Haven and its surrounds. The town's middle school, its former high school, is on Cutler Street. One of the cemetery's larger structures, in fact a small mausoleum, bears the Cutler name. Cutler had been an early Grand Haven mayor. And hadn't downtown long held a Cutler House or Cutler Hotel? One couldn't miss the Cutler name, if one had any sense of Grand Haven history. But were they all the same Cutler? And if so, was it *this* Cutler?

"Got a project?" Cutler asked Maroon, continuing to share a warm smile.

Maroon nodded before managing to utter, "Just a little thing for my wife."

"Yes, I imagine so," Cutler replied, adding, "I wasn't so handy. Business was really more my thing."

Maroon nodded again, this time taking Cutler's hint to ask, "Lumbering?"

"Yes," Cutler began, "And out of lumber, banking and development and other things. But it was the sawmills that really got me going, after a small start in mercantile."

Maroon would do his homework that night, confirming that none other than Dwight Cutler was indeed all the things Maroon had remembered, most of them generated out of Cutler's having made himself a king of Grand Haven's enormous lumber trade. His *Cutler & Savidge* partnership with another noted local timber baron milled up to 75 million feet of lumber annually, floated down the Grand River to Grand Haven. When Cutler and his fellow mill operators ran out of Michigan timber, Cutler bought land far to the north in Canada to sustain his operations. For his 1901 obituary, the *American Lumberman*, published in Chicago, called Cutler "emphatically Grand Haven's *first citizen*."

Cutler wasn't just fortuitous in coming to Grand Haven from his Massachusetts birthplace in 1848 at age 18, right at the explosion of the lumber industry. Cutler also had a knack and heart for business. He could think of nothing grander than to quietly build a thriving business and then invite the most skilled of his laborers into partnership with him to enjoy its fruits.

Cutler did exactly that, not only making himself a quiet fortune but helping many others make fortunes of their own. His Grand Haven mills sized the wood. Boats he built in his Grand Haven shipyard carried the milled lumber throughout the Midwest. And his yards in Detroit, Indianapolis, South Bend, and Michigan City, employing hundreds, sold the lumber to eager builders.

As Maroon marveled that night at Cutler's spectacular business accomplishments, he noticed that Cutler turned those accomplishments to civic good. Cutler's starting the local bank was to make capital available to industrious laborers. Cutler's building a spectacular hotel, the best in the state at the time, was to draw tourists to Grand Haven to diversify and supplement the local economy. Cutler had no political ambition but accepted the mayor's post twice, and a few other modest civic offices and duties, simply to serve skillfully and timely when called. Cutler's ambition was nothing more than to be a successful businessman, as much for others' good as for his own.

Maroon didn't know these details about Cutler early that morning at the lumber yard. But Maroon drew from Cutler's kind and humble manner that Cutler had a good heart and spirit. Cutler had blessed Grand Haven, even as the town had blessed him. His wife predeceased him, while four daughters and a son bearing his own name survived.

"You've made a good trade yourself, haven't you?" Cutler asked Maroon, before quickly correcting himself while sharing a sly smile, "Although in your line of work, you wouldn't call it a trade, rather a profession."

Maroon nodded in affirmation while returning the wry smile, in appreciation for Cutler's light humor. Lawyers and business owners tend to regard one another as distinct breeds, not always with a proper degree of respect, although each needs the other. Rix Robinson, read in law, and Martha Duncan, with a lawyer for a husband, had treated Maroon like one of their own breed. Here, though, Maroon could already see that Cutler would rather enjoy pointing out their differences.

Maroon thought of giving Cutler a comeback, but Cutler beat Maroon to the punch.

"You lawyers always have your reasons," Cutler opined with another wry smile, "While those of us in business just want to thrive."

Maroon chuckled, although shaking his head, ready to give a retort. But Cutler, a tremendously quick wit, once again beat Maroon to the punch.

"See here, though," Cutler continued, adopting a more-serious tone, "Life isn't so much about reasons or even about productivity and profit."

Maroon knew that Cutler had cut their joviality short and sensed that the time had come for Cutler to deliver his message. Indeed, Cutler continued.

"Life is instead about fitting participation," Cutler enjoined, adding, "As in constantly giving one's proportionate response."

Maroon put a hand to his mouth in thought, digesting Cutler's wisdom. He wanted to hear Cutler elaborate and illustrate but wasn't sure how not to trigger a teasing, rather than an informative, response. Cutler, though, saved Maroon the trouble, providing his own illustration.

"Both lawyers and business owners are constantly trying to solve life," Cutler explained, "When life isn't something to solve but something in which to revel with one's most apt action. Keep discerning and committing the right action with full vigor, and life's fruits abound."

Maroon nodded, observing, "You were surely a man of action."

Cutler chuckled, replying, "Likely far too much action. You know, when my hotel burned to the ground, you'd think I'd have learned my lesson. But no, I just built another one, although it wasn't quite so grand the second time around."

Maroon chuckled appreciatively at Cutler's self-deprecation. Yet rather than quickly add another witticism, Cutler paused. Maroon sensed an impending disappearance. But to Maroon's pleasant surprise, Cutler had another idea.

"Let's go pick out your wood," Cutler suggested, giving a wave of his arm to encourage Maroon to enter the long, sweet-smelling structure, in the early morning still devoid of staff or other customers.

Maroon and Cutler spent the next while pulling out, flipping over, and sighting down boards of different sizes, lengths, and woods, while Cutler expounded on their distinct features, pointed out their few defects, and extolled their many virtues. Maroon found Cutler to be a catalog of knowledge on the quarter-sawn, flat-sawn, and rift-sawn cuts and the various species, including how they would respond to sizing, sanding, finish, use, humidity, and wear. And Cutler only made a few delicious digs at lawyers along their way, friendly provocations that Maroon now managed to rebut with equal enjoyment.

Just as they had settled on a couple of choice boards for Maroon's project, Maroon looked down the length of the long building to see one of its familiar workers approaching, presumably to aid in the sale. Maroon gave a small wave of acknowledgement before turning to Cutler, hoping for a chance at their further interaction or, if not, then at least a hearty goodbye. Instead, Cutler was gone.

7

Maroon had as good a day as he'd had in a long time, completing his wife's project. He generally did woodworking in a sort of controlled fury, racing from the planing, joining, measuring, cutting, fitting, and assembly to the routing, sanding, and finishing. He wasn't one to tinker or fool around. He was a finisher, the sooner the better, as long as with reasonable care and precision. Once he got his wife's vision figuratively nailed down, Maroon was off to the races, always striving eagerly, if not madly, for the finish line.

Unless he had to allow glue or primer to dry overnight, or he ran into an unanticipated materials or design issue,

Maroon generally finished what he started in a day, come hell or high water. By day's end, Maroon could usually present the finished project to his wife, although his practice was to install it discreetly to wait for her to stumble across it.

Maroon cherished his wife's oohs and aahs over a successful project. He rued her picking at an unsuccessful project, her design of which she had thought better or the results of which just did not meet her expectations. Maroon went to great pains to work those things out ahead. He hated wasted effort and expense, especially the kind of loud, relatively dangerous, dirtying, and physically arduous effort much woodworking took. He hated even more not meeting the expectations of his beloved wife.

But the great artist, in this instance his wife, always has the prerogative of changing her mind mid-project or even post-project. Maroon had seen some of his efforts leave the house as gifts, in garage sales, or in pieces in the garbage. Others he had disassembled to use the material in the next, better-conceived or better-executed project. Maroon could at times be too proud of various work he accomplished, but not with these wood projects.

On this day, though, his wife's project went according to plan. Maroon's furious cutting, nailing, screwing, sanding, and finishing met with no significant resistance and required no significant detours, not even a second trip to the lumber yard or hardware store. Maroon's wife received the completed project with due appreciation. The executed labor had met the great artist's imagined work.

Yet the project's success wasn't what made the day so distinctly better than prior days. Maroon had successfully grumbled and raced his way through many such projects.

No, what made this day different for Maroon was Cutler's lingering presence, or more accurately, Maroon's reflections throughout the day on the time Cutler had spent with Maroon that morning.

In their planning and execution, woodworking projects generally occupied most of Maroon's mind. But not *all* of it. On these woodworking days, Maroon would often find himself ruminating over whatever recent circumstance had entertained or annoyed him, in between measurements, cuts, and other precise calculations. He raced from machine to machine in the woodworking shop, his ears covered with hearing protection and his material in hand, looking as if his full mind was on the project. But it generally wasn't. His mind was instead processing other conditions, challenges, opportunities, circumstances, or events.

On this day, though, all Maroon wanted to consider, in between the cognitive demands of the woodwork, was Cutler. Maroon had appreciated Cutler's words, his sense that one should pour one's full vigor into fitting action. Cutler had certainly done so, in the end leading a clearly spectacular and marvelously good life, in the estimation of everyone short of his few worst critics, whose negative opinions history politely buried in a landslide of favor approaching adulation.

Maroon had the vague sense that he, too, had poured himself into things at hand with adequate vigor, if not nearly with Cutler's acute business sense and surely not producing anything like similar honor or adulation. Maroon even had a good silent chuckle to himself that his racing around the woodshop, at furious work on his wife's modest project, was a fair indication of the high level of his devotion to tasks at hand, whether or not he chose the right tasks or executed them with the right actions.

Yet Maroon realized that Cutler's insights were not the greater part of Maroon's encounter that morning with the extraordinary lumberman. The greater worth of the encounter was in Cutler himself. Maroon and Cutler had in some sense communed, not over an explicit liturgy, not over bread and wine, and instead only over the most modest of household woodworking projects. But they had nonetheless communed in a sort of fractal representation of the divine liturgy.

Maroon took a deep breath with the encouraging realization, as if he were breathing Cutler in again. Cutler's spirit had the sweet smell of fresh-cut pine, the soft touch of a milled board sanded with 200-grit paper, and the satisfying sensation of sawdust in the hair after a well-wrought project.

Maroon's realization that he was breathing in Cutler, living off Cutler's gentility, acuity, and general presence through the rest of the day, gave Maroon new appreciation for the Lord's table, for communion, for that most difficult of challenges the Lord gave to consume his body and drink his blood. Maroon had fed off Cutler's spirit throughout the day, finding a surprising peace within it. Perhaps in doing so, Maroon had simultaneously communed with Cutler's Lord.

By day's end, Maroon was ready for some fresh air, to get out from under the demands of the completed project. With his feet and joints sore from the day's labor, Maroon discerned that a leisurely bike ride down to the channel would be just the refreshing thing. The sun had already fallen low enough in the western sky to hold the prospect of an entertaining sunset over the channel's waters.

As Maroon swung aboard his bike for a circuit through the cemetery on the way down to the channel, he just noticed the far-off sound of a ship's horn in the channel. A perfect ending to a nearly perfect day, Maroon thought. If the ship was coming in, then Maroon should be able to pause along the channel to watch it pass. If the ship was going out, he should be able to watch it heading off toward the horizon in the sunset.

Maroon reached the channel just as the great ship had drawn alongside the pier on its way into the harbor. To Maroon's pleasure, the ship was one of the enormous thousand-footers, dropping off road salt, loading fine dune sand for automotive casting molds, or making similar transactions at the dock a short distance upriver, just across from Harbor Island.

On some of Maroon's early morning bike excursions to Harbor Island, he would see the great ships loading or unloading in the darkness. Shipping is a 24/7 occupation, keeping at continuous work the mammoth boats and the considerable investment behind them. Even in the freezing Great Lakes winters, shipping may continue well into December and resume as early as March. Once on the waters, the boats never stop except to load or unload, when their crews are harder at work than ever.

Maroon stopped his bike, putting one foot down to balance on it, to watch the great ship pass. The sheer size of the thing impressed. Its implacable motion past the channel boardwalk impressed more. Its mammoth size relative to the narrow channel impressed even more. Ships pilots, Maroon knew, were threading a needle when entering the long, straight, and narrow channel to navigate the several curves past the downtown boardwalk and around Harbor Island to the dock.

Wind against the ship's sides, channel currents, shoals, and the ships' sheer momentum substantially increase the pilots' hazards. One great ship had recently run its bow into the steel retaining wall alongside the boardwalk. The patch in the boardwalk stands testament to the pilot's demise. The cost to repair a hull can be extravagant, not an expense for which the owners generally price their service to profit.

Maroon waved at one of the crew, standing in an opening in the great ship's side. Maroon wasn't a cheerleader, but the crew member was so close to Maroon and looked so drawn by the proximity of the dry land on which Maroon stood, balancing his bike, that it would have seemed disrespectful not to do so. The crew member waved back before turning inside the great ship, presumably to prepare for docking.

"He's got a lot to do," a voice intoned from beside Maroon.

The great ship's passing had so transfixed Maroon's attention that he hadn't noticed the elderly gentleman standing at his side.

"His captain wouldn't have liked his crew member gazing at land and waving at onlookers at such a busy and hazardous moment," the elderly gentleman resumed as he, like Maroon, watched the ship slip past.

Maroon had already discerned that the elderly gentleman represented his next otherworldly encounter. Yet the encounters had become so frequent and familiar that Maroon was in no rush to advance this one. Indeed, although the day's project had tired Maroon, and the hour was late, he hoped that this visit would linger, as the morning's visit with Cutler had.

The elderly gentleman must have read Maroon's mind. As the ship moved past and on up the channel, the gentleman observed offhandedly to Maroon, "It's a fine evening to be down by the channel. I think I'll sit for a spell. Feel free to join me."

Maroon watched as the gentleman turned slowly and a bit unsteadily, reaching for a bench along the boardwalk just behind them. The gentleman eased himself down at one end of the bench, sighed deeply, tipped his head back, and closed his eyes.

"It's just good to hear the sounds of the channel," the gentleman said quietly, eyes still closed.

Indeed, the gentleman's observation turned Maroon's attention to the low, steady hum of the great ship's engines, churning up the channel, and to the seagull cries and lapping of the water against the channel's wall, atop which stretched the boardwalk. The gentleman was right. The channel's sounds offered their own enchantment, a tiny window into the divinity beyond, in the patterns of which the channel rejoiced.

"I loved my time on these waters," the gentleman intoned. He had opened his eyes to regard Maroon once again, still perched on his bike in front of the bench.

Maroon hadn't intended to ignore the gentleman's invitation to join him on the bench. Maroon knew that he would sit with the gentleman as long as the gentleman would remain, presuming, as Maroon knew, that the gentleman was his next visitor. The channel's sounds had just captured and held Maroon's attention, as they had captured and held the gentleman's attention.

Maroon dismounted swiftly. Storing the bike behind the bench, Maroon sat at its other end opposite the elderly gentleman. He turned toward the gentleman, resting his arm along the back of the bench and waiting for the gentleman to continue. As he did so, Maroon wondered the identity of the great sea captain of the past, next to whom he now sat.

Maroon would soon learn that he sat next to Captain William Loutit, who was indeed Grand Haven's great sea captain. Many great captains piloted the tricky channel in and out of Grand Haven's port, a wonderful safe harbor from the lake's storms and other perils, except for the navigation perils the tricky channel itself held. But unlike most of those captains, who might reside in Chicago, Milwaukee, Mackinac, Bay City, Detroit, Duluth, Houghton, Sault Ste. Marie, Thunder Bay, or even Cleveland, Buffalo, and points farther east along the Great Lakes, Captain Loutit made Grand Haven his home. Loutit built an ornate, Victorian-style residence on Grand Haven's main street.

Maroon had often noticed the prominent Loutit memorial plot in the great cemetery behind his house, below the town founders' overlook. The carved-stone Loutit memorial was among the tallest, most orderly, and most elaborate of the memorials among the leading local families' plots.

The Loutit name remains prominent in and around Grand Haven due largely to the generous philanthropy of the Loutit Foundation. Captain Loutit left a substantial legacy for his son and grandson to administer. The grandson and his wife turned that legacy into the Loutit Foundation, one of the many charitable acts of which was to fund the mid-1960s construction and operation of Grand Haven's beautiful and resourceful Loutit District Library. The great captain's Loutit Foundation legacy also funded the city's community center, musical water fountain, and the popular boardwalk promenade on which Maroon and the captain right then sat.

But the great captain did even more for the community than build a gorgeous home to grace its main street and more than leave a legacy to fund key charitable improvements. When in 1871 Congress authorized the U.S. Life Saving Service, as a forerunner to the U.S. Coast Guard, Captain Loutit organized the first crew of Grand Haven lifesaving volunteers. Under the captain's direction, they built and equipped the first lifesaving station on the channel's north shore. Captain Loutit also served as the first superintendent for Michigan's twelve lifesaving stations. Grand Haven revered Captain Loutit most for saving lives on the perilous Great Lakes waters.

Maroon later recalled few specifics of the long time he spent that evening chatting with Captain Loutit. He didn't even recall the exact moment that he learned his new friend's identity. The two simply sat alongside one another, listening to the channel's sounds, enjoying the channel's sights, and giving the great captain Maroon's audience for the captain's accounts of seafaring across the Great Lakes from a Grand Haven base. Maroon could have listened to the captain for hours and in fact did.

Somewhere along the line of seafaring stories, Maroon expected Captain Loutit to impart some wisdom of the sort that the other historical figures had. Captain Loutit did not disappoint.

When the sun had set, Maroon felt a stirring to go. Indeed, he expected Captain Loutit at any moment to mysteriously return to the realm from which he had come. But a second great ship had appeared just then, making its way out of the channel. Captain Loutit and Maroon lingered in the full darkness to watch it pass.

Just before the great ship reached them, Captain Loutit had turned his storytelling to generalities, a sort of summation of his long experience on the inland seas.

"You know," the captain concluded, "My seafaring taught me that life's challenges are not health, vocation, or relationships, not even growing old, dying, or other loss."

Here, the great captain paused. He resumed just as the bow of the departing ship reached them.

"Life's challenges are instead mood, attitude, dreaming, and thinking," the captain opined in a wistful manner, adding, "My life on the seas became a gradual unburdening and lightening, learning to participate peacefully with the structure of being."

Maroon opened his mouth to make some comment of appreciation or inquiry. But before Maroon could formulate the accompanying thought, the captain suddenly pointed at the great ship's mid-deck as it passed, saying to Maroon, "Be sure to wave to the crew."

Maroon leaned forward on the bench, scanning the empty deck for the crew member or members to whom the captain had just referred. And there, Maroon finally spied an elderly gentleman leaning against the deck's rail, waving at Maroon, who waved back.

Maroon turned to grin in appreciation at the captain alongside him, but the captain had disappeared. Maroon turned back to the great ship's deck. Taking a closer look, Maroon discerned that the crew member who had waved to him from the ship's deck was none other than Captain Loutit, now laughing in delight.

Maroon watched the great captain grow smaller and harder to discern, as the massive ship hummed its stolid way out of the channel, disappearing into the black night beyond the pier's lighthouse.

8

Maroon made his way home well after nightfall, much later than his wife had expected. His leisurely bike ride down to the channel and back, ordinarily a twenty to thirty-minute excursion, had turned into a worrisome hours-long absence, for which Maroon gave no satisfying explanation to his wife. He should, in any case, have called if he was going to linger along the channel or, if not that, at least to have returned his wife's concerned texts.

Maroon thought only briefly of sharing with his wife the wonders of his long chat with Captain Loutit. But Maroon immediately banished the thought from his mind. His wife wouldn't understand the encounter and, still less, wouldn't appreciate it with interest equal to Maroon's own.

Maroon wanted to cherish the great captain's visit, not tarnish it with a spat with his rightly aggrieved wife. In the end, Maroon resolved to bear in silence whatever brunt of his wife's disfavor she deigned to administer.

For her part, Maroon's wife decided to chalk Maroon's worrying disappearance up as a sign to watch. Hadn't she noticed changes in her husband's mood? He had always been moody, even if generally cordial or even pleasant in his moodiness, if that wasn't a contradiction in terms. Maroon always seemed to try his best at keeping things light and pleasant with his wife, she generally felt, even if in his dark moods his best wasn't very good.

But lately, Maroon seemed more withdrawn, as if he was slowly disconnecting from his own household presence, even more so than having withdrawn from hers. Maroon's wife again filed away the thought under a new mental folder she had labeled *dementia*, after her husband's recent query about that very topic.

Maroon woke the next day reasonably rested, much more so than the exhaustion he had felt when waking in prior recent days. The late hour of his return home and retirement to bed may have helped, as may the fresh air sitting along the channel and stirred in his lungs on the short bike ride uphill to home.

With his wife's project finished the day before, Maroon had nothing but writing to do for the day. And well ahead on his writing assignments, Maroon felt little pressure to figuratively hammer away. He would thus take the day as it came, with writing as a backdrop to keep him engaged.

Maroon puttered through the morning, rising frequently from his writing to empty the dishwasher, answer the door, get the mail, fold the laundry, bring the emptied garbage cans in from the curb, let the dogs in and out, and do other light household chores. The frequent movement helped relieve his writing posture, stimulate his mind, and, most of all, restore his wife's favor. Maroon had been wary of the deleterious impact of his previous evening's absence.

About midday, Maroon's daughter and young grandson paid an impromptu visit. And no sooner had they arrived, than the young tyke wanted to hike through the cemetery woods. At his daughter's urging, Maroon joined them.

With no particular direction in mind, they headed generally west through the cemetery, toward the imposing, forested dunes rising high between the cemetery and the great lake. But Maroon had learned that hiking along the cemetery's asphalt roads or its settled pedestrian shortcuts and trails was never enough for his grandson's hyperactive energy. The child wanted to go straight up the great dune, deep into the forest.

Maroon protested lightly, suggesting more congenial alternatives. But grandson overruled Maroon's objection. Groaning inwardly, Maroon began the slow slog up the steep dune, over and around fallen tree trunks, often holding onto standing tree trunks for balance. Grandson and daughter followed him up.

Maroon had hiked these woods with his wife and alone on rare occasions. If one didn't mind the strenuous exertion and a bit of wandering about, they offered a more-direct route to the beach than the circuitous route along the cemetery's paved roads. Maroon soon suggested that they make their way along a trail he knew would lead them to the beach overlook. Once again, though, grandson overruled. They would instead wander about without aim other than to enjoy the woods' depths.

Deeper into the woods, they began catching glimpses of the cottages of the Highland Park Association. The woods through which Maroon, his daughter, and his grandson were wandering had a fascinating history of their own.

Grand Haven's founders and first families would inevitably turn their attention from trapping, trading, settlement, and lumbering to family life and recreation, stimulated by an emerging tourism trade. Grand Haven's gorgeous natural setting and temperate summer weather, cooled by lakefront breezes, naturally attracted summer residents, visitors, and tourists. The town's year-round residents benefited from that summer trade, as they continue to do. But Grand Haven needed places to house the summer residents and guests.

The forested dunes through which Maroon and his family hiked that day provided the location for the town's first concerted solution for summer housing. The town's residents extended the avenue that already headed south out of town, further south and then due west to the lakeshore. Its terminus among the lakefront dunes became the Highland Park Association, where resident and non-resident families built their summer cottages.

The Highland Park Association incorporated in 1886 as a conservation district, to enable families to construct up to 100 cottages on land the city owned and leased to the association for that purpose. Families had been tenting in the dunes for many years already, marking the spot as sufficiently accessible and conducive for summer residence.

Grand Haven

Grand Haven had already burgeoned as a tourist and summer destination beginning in 1871, when mercantilist W.C. Sheldon discovered mineral springs in the city's downtown. *W.C. Sheldon's Magnetic Mineral Springs* drew visitors to the springs for their claimed health effects, gained by both drinking and bathing. When many years later the emporium closed, the city moved Sheldon's grand fountain from the site to the nearby Central Park, where the fountain remains today.

More-or-less-original Highland Park cottages among the woods also remain today. Signs advertising their late-1800s origin hang from the walls of a few. Others burned or decayed to the point of destruction, while others gave way to improved residences, even a few habitable year round.

Maroon, though, had tired of forging his way up and down the steep and heavily wooded dunes. He waved his daughter and grandson ahead for whatever further explorations they wished to make. He would wait for their return by the easier avenue route. Maroon made his way around to the avenue, to sit and rest on a low wall in front of one of the old cottages.

Seeing an elderly woman approaching along the avenue's slim sidewalk, Maroon smiled up at her and pulled his legs in to let her pass.

"Tires one out hiking these dunes, doesn't it?" she said, as she paused before passing along the narrow sidewalk and on toward the lake overlook just ahead.

Maroon nodded noncommittally. He hadn't meant to interrupt the elderly woman's pleasant walk, and he was too bushed even for pleasant conversation.

"I remember when my home here was the first in the new park," the woman continued, despite Maroon's attempt to get her to pass on.

The elderly woman's comment triggered a flood of regret in Maroon. He looked up respectfully at the spry elderly woman standing before him, sharing a smile of regret, as he eased his weary body up from his seat on the low wall.

"This home was yours?" Maroon asked in reply, motioning toward the small cottage on the low wall of which he had perched.

"Yes," she replied with a look of homesteader's pride, "Built in 1887, the year the city leased us the land, as you can see from the owner's sign."

Maroon had long ago noted the small sign on this cottage and similar signs on several others along this stretch of the avenue, which he walked, biked, and even drove on frequent occasions. He knew the antiquity of some of these cottages.

"Two others came right after mine, that same summer," the elderly woman continued, adding, "And within ten years we had about fifty of them spread up the dunes in the woods."

"What was it like here then?" Maroon asked respectfully, with genuine interest. The woman's appearance was swiftly abating his weariness.

"Pretty rustic, as it was when we tented here at first," the woman replied, "Although as our numbers grew, our amusements multiplied."

Maroon listened as the elderly woman described some of those multiplying amusements. They included a water-walking machine, parachute leap, and hot-air-balloon demonstration. Moving pictures came in 1902. The entertaining figure Captain Jack maintained a pavilion on the beach from which one could rent a swimsuit by the hour and a pier into the lake from which one could fish. Residents set up tennis courts on the lawns.

Highland Park eventually hosted other, grander edifices and events, well beyond the original tents, first humble cottages, and their modest amusements. The grand and elaborately decorated Highland Park Hotel opened its twenty-five rooms along the beach below in 1890. One lot holder, a noted Grand Rapids architect, erected the spectacular Highland Castle in 1897, festooned with turrets, gingerbread, and cathedral glass. Facilitating further development, the city connected Highland Park to the city's water system in 1895. In another five years, Highland Park gained the city's electric lights. Telephones fell in between.

When the elderly woman mentioned tennis courts, Maroon asked about the magical Highland Park Tennis Club hidden deep in a glen within the woods. Maroon had discovered the place walking over one of the wooded dunes. It had burst upon him then as if it had descended from above, dropped like a gem among the surrounding sylvan dunes. The woman proudly explained that the club, replacing the original grass courts, had hosted national-level junior tennis tournaments in the 1920s and 1930s. Highland Park was a destination place, drawing regular visitors and cottage owners from Chicago, St. Louis, and other distant parts.

Throughout the elderly woman's friendly chatter, though, Maroon held the misgiving that he had not asked or discerned her name. Maroon presumed that she knew him. Why else would she come from her other realm, stopping on the spot to give him a history lesson? Maroon knew a little of the history of Highland Park. The elderly woman had disclosed much more of it than Maroon had ever imagined. But she had given no clue to her identity other than as the owner of the first cottage.

No sooner had Maroon opened his mouth intending the awkward effort of asking his new friend's name, than the woman blurted out, "Oh, by the way, I'm Sarah Benedict Rhines Saunders."

Mrs. Saunders extended her right hand delicately. Maroon took it gently, giving it the lightest squeeze of kind acknowledgment.

"Hey, Papa!" another voice called to Maroon from just up the sidewalk toward the lake.

Maroon turned to see his daughter and grandson making their way slowly toward him, his grandson trailing, finally exhausted.

"Excuse me," Maroon said, turning back to Mrs. Saunders. Tipping his head toward the two figures making their way toward them, he explained, "My daughter and grandson back from their walk."

Maroon had expected Mrs. Saunders to have disappeared. Instead, Mrs. Saunders still stood before Maroon, smiling broadly as she watched the two figures draw near.

"With whom were you talking?" Maroon's daughter asked as she reached Maroon to wait for Maroon's grandson to catch up. Maroon's daughter seemed oblivious to Mrs. Saunders, standing right beside her.

While Maroon's daughter turned to call to his grandson to hurry up, Maroon looked at Mrs. Saunders, who raised her eyebrows and shrugged, with a twinkle in her eye and a growing smile.

"Umm, no one?" Maroon answered his daughter.

"Oh," his daughter replied, "It looked like you were speaking with someone, but I didn't see anyone."

Maroon shrugged, stealing another glance at Mrs. Saunders, whose smile back at Maroon broadened.

Maroon shook his head in confused astonishment.

"You alright?" his daughter asked.

"Just a little lightheaded," Maroon replied.

"Want me to go get the car?" she offered.

"No, no," Maroon replied, "I'll be fine."

Maroon's grandson had joined them. Grandson and daughter led the way up the avenue toward the cemetery entrance route back to Maroon's home. Maroon and Mrs. Saunders walked along behind, Maroon in the odd position of trying to ignore Mrs. Saunders, for his daughter's purposes, while trying to acknowledge Mrs. Saunders' presence, for Mrs. Saunders' own sake. Yet once again, Mrs. Saunders read Maroon's mind.

"Don't worry about me," Mrs. Saunders said to Maroon, "I'll just walk along with you for a spell until we finish our conversation."

Maroon nodded an acknowledgment while glancing ahead at his daughter. Maroon's daughter continued walking gaily on, now holding her exhausted young son's hand to keep him moving resolutely forward. Maroon's daughter hadn't heard a word Mrs. Saunders said to Maroon, even though Mrs. Saunders was walking right behind her.

"You know," Mrs. Saunders resumed in a cheerful voice, "I was so glad that my husband agreed that we should build the first cottage out here."

Once again, Maroon nodded.

Maroon's daughter shot a glance over her shoulder at Maroon, asking, "You alright, Papa?"

Maroon nodded, smiling weakly while trying not to look at Mrs. Saunders walking beside him.

"Are you finding your quiet time, Maroon?" Mrs. Saunders asked.

Maroon took a deep breath to reply but, thinking of his daughter just ahead of him, merely nodded, while emitting a muffled, "Mm-hmm."

Maroon's daughter shot another glance back at Maroon, who cleared his throat with a sound similar to his muffled reply to Mrs. Saunders, trying to conceal his insufficiently discrete communication with the otherworldly figure walking beside him.

"Well, do keep trying," Mrs. Saunders continued to address Maroon pleasantly, "Our time here is so brief that we should give less attention to demands and more attention to opportunities."

Maroon nodded, clearing his throat again as a sign of appreciation for Mrs. Saunders' wisdom. Maroon's daughter shot him another glance, shaking her head to indicate her concern for him. Maroon shrugged, shaking his head back at her to indicate that he was fine.

"I think I'll turn back now," Mrs. Saunders announced to Maroon, "But it was so good to meet you and share this cottage discourse with you."

Mrs. Saunders gave Maroon a little wave of her delicate hand before peeling off from their little group and turning around to head back up the avenue past her little cottage toward the lake.

Maroon glanced over his shoulder once, seeing Mrs. Saunders in a pleasant retreat. He glanced over his shoulder a second time moments later, and she had disappeared.

"Are you sure you're alright?" Maroon's daughter asked him over her shoulder, having noticed Maroon's glances back up the avenue.

"I'll be fine once we get home," Maroon answered, admitting his present weakness. The situation's otherworldly duality had indeed strained Maroon to the breaking point.

9

"Papa's acting kind of strange," Maroon's daughter whispered to Maroon's wife in a quiet moment after their return from the Highland Park hike. Maroon and his grandson had retired to the office to watch cartoons and recover from the hike.

Maroon's wife raised her eyebrows in response, waiting for his daughter to explain.

"He was talking to himself," the daughter whispered.

Maroon's wife tipped her head and shrugged, replying without expressing any concern, "He's been distracted. I'll watch him. Let me know if you see anything else."

In fact, though, Maroon's wife was concerned. She didn't want her daughter to worry. The episodes might pass. But she, too, had detected changes in her husband, beyond his absence the prior night.

Maroon sat at his office desk considering what had just happened, while his grandson lay on the couch watching cartoons. The hike had produced a close encounter of another sort.

Initially, Maroon's otherworldly visits had been brief and entirely isolated. He could easily keep them to himself because they occurred out of sight and lasted only moments. They had of course shocked Maroon, undermining what he thought about the nature of the world. Maroon, like at least half of the rest of the billions of people around the world, acknowledged the possibility of a higher realm. He even accepted that the higher realm might hold a way for personality to persist. He didn't give it a tremendous amount of thought and instead accepted the conventional Christian position, but he expected to have some sort of existence of his own after his earthly demise.

Yet he had never seriously considered the possibility of visitations from that dimension. Of course, he was familiar with popular speculations and representations of such visitations. He had, for instance, read Charles Dickens' *A Christmas Carol* and seen the film and television representations of the story of Ebenezer Scrooge, visited by Marley's ghost and other figures from beyond. And when he thought of it, he could recall several other fictional or assertedly authentic accounts of such visitations. But he hadn't given general or specific credit to those accounts.

Like other reasonable people, Maroon had accepted the fictional accounts as entertainment, disbelieved the most preposterous of the accounts claimed as authentic, and suspended judgment as to the rest. When friends had intimated their own experiences or quietly related experiences by trusted others, Maroon had listened respectfully, mentally filing their accounts away for later, without ever having returned to them for more-serious reflection.

Maroon was aware that a scholar without a clear stake in the question had recently compiled a multi-volume work of accounts of the otherworldly and miraculous down through the ages, from ancient times to today. Maroon was also aware that the scholar's conclusion was that the accounts reflected more than mass psychosis, traditions handed down, or individual overactive imaginations. But once again, Maroon had mentally filed the information away for future consideration.

When the schoolchildren disappeared with Miss White, though, Maroon had a broader reckoning to navigate. Then, when Cutler had lingered to help Maroon pick out wood for his wife's project, Maroon had yet more otherworldly influence to integrate. When Captain Loutit had regaled Maroon with seafaring stories into the night, Maroon had even more of the higher realm's meddling to traverse. But when Mrs. Saunders continued to interact with Maroon in the presence of Maroon's unwitting daughter and grandson, the encounters had crossed a line. They had shattered Maroon's world.

As his grandson watched cartoons from the couch, behind which Maroon sat slouched at his desk, Maroon finally and fully accepted that the world wasn't constructed as he had forever assumed. The cosmos was instead far more dynamic, a twin engine of lower and higher realms with substantial possibility for open influence and interaction. The cosmos was precisely as the most traditional ancient view expressed it. Maroon's modern suspension of belief, not the traditional view of resurrected souls, was the figment of imagination. Maroon was in a new world of incredible possibility.

"A commercial, Papa," Maroon's grandson interrupted Maroon's musings, "Can you fix it?"

Maroon fiddled with the television's remote control until he had skipped the commercial, restoring the cartoons for his grandson's enjoyment.

The afternoon's remainder passed with a comforting degree of normality. Maroon needed it. So did his wife, daughter, and grandson. An enchanted world's solace is its tediousness. Folding the laundry, picking weeds out of the flowers, and sweeping the driveway make living in an enchanted world possible, when the enchantments shatter the mind.

Maroon was relieved to have a volunteer matter to which to attend the next day. He needed an ordinary encounter to balance the extraordinary encounters of the several prior days. After a quiet morning of writing, Maroon headed to the local Christian school, where his daughter taught and his grandson attended preschool, for a midday building committee meeting. Maroon helped the school as a volunteer wherever he could, including on legal matters.

Grand Haven

Grand Haven Christian School is one of the older continuously operated private Christian grade schools in the country. Maroon had gradually come to learn of its deep connection with the community that it so well represented.

Education had been important to Grand Haven since the day of the town's founding, including education in the divine origin of the gorgeous lands the residents inherited and inhabited, and from which they so richly drew. Reverend Ferry and his sister-in-law Mary White saw to that commitment to the education of all, after the will and in the spirit of the cosmos' creator. Miss White didn't just educate young men, after the fashion of the day, but also young women, tradesmen, seafarers, homemakers, and all other comers.

Grand Haven Christian School inherited that commitment when in 1880 its African-American landlord Mr. Smith opened the school's doors to the hard-pressed Dutch immigrants who didn't even speak English. The school instructed in Dutch in its early years. Today, it instructs in English but offers a Spanish-immersion option for children to learn in that language from preschool through eighth grade. All should have access to education, including education that recognizes the intersection between the world we see and the realm of which we only know.

Having arrived early for the meeting, Maroon sat in his truck in the parking lot, window down to the pleasant breeze, while thumbing through preparatory notes on his cell phone.

"Pleasant day," someone greeted Maroon through his open window.

Maroon looked up from his cell phone to see a distinguished-looking gentleman standing alongside the truck, shielding his eyes from the sun to look toward the bright but empty school, in the serene silence of its summer vacation.

"Quite a difference from when school's in session," the gentleman said, with a sweep of his arm around the parking lot, empty except for the principal's vehicle.

"Are you here for the building meeting?" Maroon asked, not recognizing the gentleman. The building committee regularly met with architects, landscapers, and contractors, of which Maroon assumed his distinguished visitor was one.

"Oh, I've done my share of meetings," the gentleman replied with a slight groan and chuckle, in which Maroon joined. After a pause, the gentleman added, "Let's just say I'm here to observe."

And that was it. Maroon's eyes opened to his next otherworldly encounter. He breathed a silent sigh, hoping that it would prove more manageable than the prior day's visitation.

"You know," the gentleman observed with a far-off look, "My girl's institute, rather than my professional practice, business interests, or civic offices, turned out to be my life's work."

The gentleman turned to Maroon, who still sat in his truck, to gauge his reaction. Maroon looked blankly back, having no sense yet of the gentleman's identity.

"Oh," the gentleman interrupted himself, "I'm sorry. I should introduce myself."

Extending a hand up to the truck's open window, the gentleman said, "Healy Akeley, Maroon. My girl's institute was the Akeley Institute, although most called it the *Akeley School for Girls*."

Maroon took Akeley's hand, giving it as good of a shake as he could manage through the window. Maroon knew the Akeley name. He was disappointed not to recall ever having heard of the Akeley School for Girls.

In his research that night, Maroon was astonished to discover that Grand Haven's own Akeley School for Girls had been a local pillar and to some degree a regional or even national standard for the instruction of young women for a period of a half century. The Akeley Institute attracted young women from near and far for the breadth, depth, and high quality of its instruction, from the 1870s to 1928, when it graduated its last class and closed its doors. Its rich educational ministry ended only after public schools had gradually opened their doors and improved instruction for girls.

Maroon knew the Akeley name from the proud family memorial lifted high in the grand cemetery behind his house, among the other notable family plots. Maroon also knew the Akeley name from the beautifully restored 1870s Akeley Building in downtown Grand Haven, with its historical marker. For its century and a half of vibrant life, the building had hosted law offices, dry goods stores, department stores, tailor shops, and a bazaar, serving and supplying the local population.

Maroon's research also revealed how Healy Akeley had managed to fund his beloved Akeley School for Girls, even leaving it a legacy to continue long after his 1912 death. Akeley came to Grand Haven from Massachusetts in 1858, already trained in law. Interrupted by a few years of military service as a Civil War captain, Akeley put his Grand Haven law practice to good use, discerning business opportunities and forming partnerships. Before long, Akeley owned and operated a shipbuilding company, sawmill, lumber yard, and one of the world's largest shingle suppliers. Akeley's ships, built in his own shipyard, distributed his shingles, milled in his sawmill, across the full reaches of the Great Lakes. His vertically integrated businesses made fortunes for Akeley and his equally noteworthy partners Hackley, Hume, Boyden, and Kirby.

Akeley also took his turn at civic duties, like other local business owners and professionals before and after him. After his officer service in the Civil War, Akeley accepted President Grant's appointment as Michigan's customs collector, an office he carried for nearly a decade and a half while building and guiding his businesses. Akeley then served as Grand Haven's mayor. He was also a substantial supporter of local churches. Grand Haven's richly integrated commercial, charitable, civic, and spiritual culture influenced and guided Akeley, just as it influenced and guided so many other notable Grand Haven figures. Akeley was another marvel of his lakeshore environment.

Maroon knew little of this history when greeting Akeley in the school parking lot. But Maroon could tell from the way that Akeley spoke and carried himself that Akeley was a person of insight and accomplishment.

"Professional practice was satisfying and business alluring," Akeley mused as he squinted in the sun outside Maroon's truck, "But educating those young women, to fit them for their best place in the world, now *that* was worthwhile."

Akeley shook his head gently in wonder, beaming, before adding to Maroon, "I suppose you feel the same way about this school and your educator daughter."

Maroon nodded.

Maroon learned from his research that night that the Akeley Institute didn't just teach girls to cook, sew, and make and keep a home, although those skills constituted a profound vocation. The Akeley School for Girls also taught young women writing, mathematics, and several foreign languages, and to play basketball, tennis, and golf. The Akeley Institute also helped young women develop their talents for the arts, as vocalists, musicians, dancers, and dramatic actors. The Akeley Institute had both dedicated staff and visiting artists training the girls in their greatest interests and strongest talents. Akeley Institute graduates went on to college to become lawyers, judges, journalists, and missionaries., at a time when such opportunities were rare for women.

Akeley also ensured that the local community benefited from his girls' school. The Akeley Institute hosted costume parties, musicals, plays, and other social and cultural events, specifically for the public, often attracting professional performers and renowned lecturers from Chicago and other distant parts, drawn by Grand Haven's fine summer weather and social life.

Maroon was coming to appreciate more and more how vital a sound school can be in supporting the needs and ambitions of the families who send their students to it. Maroon was also seeing more of how a vital school contributes to a community's health and welfare. He had been an educator at the professional level for half of his professional career. He knew the difference a strong educational institution and higher education program can make. But the contributions of a school helping younger, maturing students develop good character, now *that* was truly a difference maker.

"Hey," Akeley interjected, "Don't you have to be getting to your meeting?"

A couple of other vehicles had already arrived, their occupants making their way into the school. Maroon took a quick look at his watch. Indeed, he had to get going. Akeley stepped back and watched as Maroon gathered himself to slip from the truck and head across the parking lot to the school's door.

"Mind if I come along?" Akeley asked.

Akeley's suggestion both relieved Maroon of the quandary of how to politely and fruitfully end his so-far-brief encounter with Akeley, while introducing a new complication. As helpful as Akeley might be in a building committee meeting, Maroon had no place or position to invite him. And how would Maroon even introduce Akeley? *Meet my new friend from the last century?*

But then it dawned on Maroon. Akeley, like Mrs. Saunders the day before, would surely be invisible to the meeting's other participants. Maroon's only challenge would be managing the dual but non-intersecting relationships. He would have to do his best, better than he had done with his daughter and Mrs. Saunders the prior day.

"By all means, join me," Maroon replied to Akeley, as graciously as Maroon could manage after his brief frantic calculations.

The two men sauntered together across the parking lot and to and through the school's open door. Along their way, Akeley chatted cordially, sharing bits and pieces of his experience with the girls' institute. Maroon tried to stifle his nods and verbal responses, conscious that anyone watching him might think he was talking to himself.

The building meeting proceeded in the same fashion. Akeley took a seat in the conference room's corner, unnoticed by the others. Maroon kept his attention on the others, avoiding looking at or addressing Akeley. Akeley ventured only a few, well-timed, quiet utterances to Maroon during the meeting's course. Maroon tried to avoid acknowledging Akeley's brief interjections, although Maroon used a couple of them to make his own insightful points, advancing the business of the meeting.

The meeting soon ended, to Maroon's great relief. Maroon made his way out as quickly as he could do so, without seeming rushed or insolent. Akeley slipped out with Maroon, following Maroon across the parking lot toward his truck. Along the way, Akeley shared his summary thoughts.

"You all have a good vision for the school," Akeley encouraged Maroon warmly, adding, "One always has to be looking as far forward as one can, and your leadership seems to be doing so."

Maroon so deeply appreciated Akeley's words and was so relieved over escaping the meeting without an obvious lapse in his handling of the dual relationships, that Maroon momentarily forgot himself. Having reached his truck, Maroon stopped, turned to Akeley, extended his hand, and said with equal warmth, "So good to have had this time with you."

Akeley smiled back, taking and shaking Maroon's hand before Maroon turned to climb into his truck. When Maroon looked back in Akeley's direction, he was gone. Beyond where Akeley had stood, Maroon noticed two committee members staring curiously at him. Maroon didn't notice his daughter's car, parked in the shade behind him.

10

Maroon spent the rest of the day trying to keep to himself in his office. He needed recovery time. Things were getting progressively more complicated. Maroon wondered where the peculiar encounters might soon head. He tried not to think about it, presuming instead that they would soon naturally subside.

Maroon's daughter and grandson stopped by the house late that afternoon for the little tyke to spend some time with grandma, his *Ná*, as he had adoringly called her from his first efforts to express her name. Maroon greeted them cordially before slipping back to his office.

Maroon's daughter tipped her head in Maroon's direction after he had disappeared, while saying to Maroon's wife, "He was acting strange again at the school this afternoon."

"Really?" Maroon's wife replied, as she hugged her grandson.

"Talking to himself again, like yesterday on our walk," Maroon's daughter confirmed.

Maroon's grandson piped up, "Papa was talking to a lady behind us as we walked."

"No one else was walking with us, Son," Maroon's daughter corrected the little guy, who simply turned away from his mom, ignoring the correction while hugging his grandma again.

"The groundskeeper told me when we stopped by the school on our way over here," Maroon's daughter explained to Maroon's wife, adding, "We saw it, too. We had just pulled up and hadn't gotten out yet. He even pretended to shake someone's hand."

"Papa wasn't pretending," Maroon's grandson interjected, adding, "The man shook his hand back."

"Let's not play games, Son," his mom corrected him. As the dogs scooted past in excitement at the company, she added, "Why don't you give them a biscuit."

The little guy hurried off, chattering at the dogs to get their attention for biscuits.

Maroon's daughter looked at Maroon's wife, waiting for a reply to her doubly concerning disclosure. Maroon's wife pursed her lips, trying to think of something satisfactory but not alarming. Nothing came to mind.

"Thanks, Honey," Maroon's wife finally said. Changing the subject, she added, "What do you think our little guy wants to do? If he's tired, he and I can watch cartoons in the bedroom while you take a walk."

"But what about Dad?" Maroon's daughter persisted.

Maroon's wife shrugged, shaking her head. Turning to chase after her grandson, she replied only, "We'll play with the dogs. I'll feed him if he's hungry. You take a walk."

Maroon's daughter made her way to the office. Opening the door, she slipped in and took a seat on the couch, in front of where Maroon sat slouched at his desk, staring blankly at the computer screen.

After a little small talk, to which Maroon responded curtly but appropriately, his daughter asked, "You alright?"

Maroon nodded blankly. Stumbling for words, he finally said, "Just need a little quiet time."

Taking the hint, his daughter rose to slip out. Maroon winced. Realizing that he had sounded too off-putting, he added, "Let me know if you two go for a walk, and I'll join you."

Maroon's daughter smiled and nodded at him, as she closed the door behind her. Maroon let out another sigh of relief. He appreciated his daughter's concern. She was always thoughtful. But her concern was only adding to Maroon's increasing urgency to find a way to manage, or perhaps even to end, the otherworldly encounters that, although marvelous, were threatening to completely upend his world.

For the first time, Maroon wondered whether he wanted the encounters to simply end, never to return. Initially, his entire effort had been to make sense of the encounters. After the first one, he had assumed it would be the only one. After the second and third, he had assumed that they would be few, brief, manageable, and soon over. But as the encounters grew longer and more complex,

Maroon could see how threatening they were to his ability to appear sane and act sensibly in his own world.

Maroon knew that some people wait a lifetime for a visitation from beyond, whether by a departed loved one, a wise saint, or an angel. Indeed, some hope for any kind of apparition from beyond, either to entertain their fancy, engage their imagination, or give some kind of hope to their desperately empty world. And yet here, Maroon had appearance after appearance, only to begin to believe that he would have been better off without any of them.

Maroon's silent reasoning gradually led him to the conclusion that the divine realm must largely remain hidden, if humankind was going to have any hope of navigating their own realm in a stable fashion. Those who scoff at the idea of the divine realm take its invisibility as proof of its non-existence, Maroon recognized. But perhaps, he thought, its invisibility is further proof of its existence. If the divine realm is more or less as tradition holds it to be, then it must not interact openly with the earthly realm, Maroon concluded. If it did so, we'd be living in more disaster, not less disaster.

Maroon had also gradually come to a broader and perhaps deeper understanding of the divine realm's nature. Yes, the realm beyond might well be populated with angels, saints, and in its nether reaches demons and unredeemed sinners. But even before his first otherworldly encounter, just days earlier, Maroon had been gaining a new appreciation that the other realm need not necessarily admit of containing winged infants or harp-bearing young women in gossamer dress, not the least ghouls and apparitions.

Maroon had already come to the conclusion that the realm beyond wasn't simply another world like our own, with a peculiar wall separating the two. It was instead *different*, yes higher, but not simply in the sense of being somewhere *up in the sky*. The divine realm was instead rarefied. It was transformed and transformative. It was the essence and highest nature of what Maroon encountered every day.

The figures from beyond who had recently graced Maroon's world, while simultaneously upending it, had shown him that they were indeed already present around him in the core, meat, or marrow of what Maroon saw, heard, thought, and did. And they weren't merely the essential of the earth's baser things. They were also the target, goal, purpose, and end of earthly things.

Maroon guessed that the figures who had visited him were not actually the highest of things above. He guessed that they had stooped quite a bit to reach a lower level, which was the highest level that he could comprehend. Maroon guessed that if the figures had visited him in their fullest divine form, or had sent the superior to whom they answered above them, the encounter wouldn't have just upended Maroon's world but instead have utterly shattered it. Maroon would not have been able to continue. His daughter would have found him in a pool on the floor of his office, rather than slouching in his chair, trying to make sense of things far above him, showing themselves to him in barely manageable but wholly gracious bits.

"Hey, Pa," Maroon's daughter broke his train of thought as she opened the office door again, "Want to join us at the waterfront? We thought we might try to board the Coast Guard ships, if our little guy here is up to it."

Maroon's grandson pushed his way past his mom and into the office, to flop on the couch.

"Do you want to watch cartoons with Papa?" Maroon's daughter asked the little guy, who shook his head.

"So you want to go see the boats?" Maroon's daughter asked him instead, receiving an affirmative nod.

Maroon gave the little guy a thumbs up, receiving thumbs up in return. An hour later, after a hike through the cemetery and other woods, Maroon, his daughter, and his grandson were standing along the channel, gazing up at the largest of the Coast Guard ships moored along the channel.

Grand Haven has long claimed the title *Coast Guard City U.S.A.* Captain Loutit had his own significant role in laying the groundwork for that appellation, with his work in bringing a lifesaving station to the town while directing other lifesaving stations around the lakefront perimeter of the state's Lower Peninsula. Those lifesaving stations, including the one in Grand Haven, became Coast Guard stations when Congress created the military branch in 1915 out of the U.S. Revenue Cutter Service and U.S. Life-Saving Service.

Congress recently began designating Coast Guard Cities, allowing the service's commandant to share the recognition with dozens of other cities, coast to coast and inland, that support Coast Guard stations and their families. But Grand Haven was the first designee, as Congress explicitly provided. Grand Haven lost its title to Cleveland as a Coast Guard district headquarters, in the service's 1939 reorganization. But Grand Haven continued to host a Coast Guard cutter, significant service station, and iconic lighthouse. And its annual Coast Guard festival brought not just parades and other celebrations but also several Coast Guard vessels to moor along the channel for public viewing.

Maroon's daughter and grandson stood in line to board the largest of the vessels, a cutter. Maroon begged off, the hike having already exhausted him. He instead took a seat on a bench in Escanaba Park, a small memorial grounds along the channel, beside the Coast Guard station. Throngs milled the grounds, including many families with children excited by the grand boats flying their many, brightly colored insignia flags. Maroon watched as his daughter and grandson reached the head of the line and walked up the gangway to board the cutter.

"Quite a sight, isn't it?" a voice addressed Maroon from behind the bench on which he sat.

The hair on the back of Maroon's neck tingled with the next encounter's numinosity. Maroon turned to regard his otherworldly visitor, who leaned heavily on the back of the bench on which Maroon sat.

"Mind if I get off these aching feet?" asked the older, thicker man, doubtless an ox-strong and hardy soul when of younger years.

Maroon smiled wanly at the man, motioning to the vacant seat beside him and saying, "Be my guest."

While Maroon forced a note of kindness, he could tell that his guest had detected Maroon's sardonic tone, for the man replied, "I won't trouble you with mindless chatter, nor interrupt your family time. I can see you're just catching your breath until your next round with your daughter and grandson."

The man motioned to Maroon's daughter, who was just then helping Maroon's grandson step from the gangway onto the cutter's deck. Maroon said nothing, only nodding his appreciation for the man's sensitivity, while wondering how much the man knew of Maroon and his family.

"I just wanted to make my brief annual visit to the memorial," the man continued, making a sweep of his arm around Escanaba Park, where the salvaged yardarm of the sunken cutter *Escanaba* stood, behind signs and plaques commemorating the lives lost in the cutter's World War II sinking.

For a moment, Maroon wondered whether he had mistaken an ordinary visitor for a resident of the realm beyond. But Maroon's preliminary estimation, signaled by the hair on the back of his neck, had been correct, as Maroon's visitor promptly revealed.

"I lost many friends in the *Escanaba*'s sinking," the man resumed, after a respectful pause. He added, "I'd have been lost, too, if my clothes hadn't frozen to the debris to which I was clinging."

The thick, older man paused, turning to Maroon with an extended hand, and saying, "O'Malley's the name. Sorry to bore you, when I said I'd be no bother."

Maroon instantly took and heartily shook O'Malley's offered hand, the immense strength of which caused no small amount of pain in Maroon's too-eager grip. On O'Malley's release, Maroon retracted his hand to massage away the pinch O'Malley's vise grip had caused. But O'Malley ignored his unintentional offense to continue on with his account.

"The rescuers pulled me aboard unconscious, with only one other survivor," the man resumed, concluding his brief account, with which Maroon was already reasonably familiar, with, "We lost 103 good men that day, many of them from right around here."

A submarine torpedo or drifting mine must have caused the *Escanaba*'s swift sinking after a waterline burst of flames along its hull. Two other ships in the convoy the *Escanaba* was escorting through the North Atlantic saw the flames and came for instant rescue, despite that the *Escanaba* had no time to send a distress signal. It was gone within a couple of minutes.

Although built in a different Michigan city and named after yet another Michigan city, the *Escanaba* made Grand Haven's Coast Guard station her home from her first commissioning, breaking ice and performing search and rescue in beloved service on the Great Lakes, out of her idyllic home port. O'Malley was right in calling Maroon's attention to the enormous local Grand Haven loss when the cutter went down.

As Maroon listened to O'Malley's account, Maroon's daughter stood with Maroon's grandson high on the cutter's bridge, waving to Maroon far below on the bench, trying in vain to get his attention. "Wave to Papa," she urged Maroon's grandson, who joined in the fun.

"Hah!" Maroon's daughter finally said in humorous frustration, "Papa's talking to himself again."

Maroon's grandson mumbled, "He's not talking to himself. He's talking to the man beside him."

But Maroon's daughter, accustomed to her son's lately too-frequent contradiction of many little things she said, ignored his comment, chalking it up to the little guy's *momma's always wrong* phase.

Back on the bench, O'Malley was already preparing to take his leave of Maroon, saying, "Look here, I'd better get going. Your daughter and grandson are making their way down now from the bridge. Did you see them waving to you?"

Maroon winced. The immediacy of O'Malley's horrific account, which Maroon had several times before already imagined on these Escanaba Park visits, had distracted him from the progress of his daughter and grandson. If they had waved to Maroon from the bridge, they would have surely seen him listening to the thick seaman, although Maroon presumed that they would not have seen the seaman at all. Maroon was in trouble again. He knew it.

O'Malley had already risen from the bench to make his way off. Maroon glanced toward the cutter, wary of acknowledging O'Malley's departure, lest his daughter observe him talking again to thin air.

"You know," O'Malley observed, while arching his back and stretching his neck to get everything back in order before ambling away, "You've got treasures in those two."

Motioning again toward the cutter, down the gangway of which Maroon's daughter and grandson were now making their way, O'Malley added, "Hold onto them tightly but not too tightly. If my rescue from those frigid waters taught me anything, it's that life is a lot about getting the right grip."

O'Malley smiled warmly at Maroon, who could not resist looking up at him with a warm smile back. O'Malley's words had softened Maroon's heart for his daughter and grandson to the point that he no longer cared whether they saw him conversing with an imaginary, but also very real, figure.

11

"Pretty impressive, huh?" Maroon greeted his daughter and grandson as they made their way off the Coast Guard cutter. He hugged the little guy.

"Yes, from down here," his daughter agreed, "Although on board, it's like a sardine can."

Maroon nodded with a smile and chuckle, replying, "Ready for the hike back?"

"We might need some ice cream first," Maroon's daughter shared, assessing, "He's flagging badly, the poor little guy."

The small party enjoyed further respite on Maroon's bench, while his grandson consumed ice cream requisitioned from the nearby shop along the boardwalk. The supplies worked. The little guy made the long trek back home through the woods and cemetery with extraordinary aplomb, considering his young age and diminutive stature. His mom carried him piggyback only a little of the way.

The outing earned Maroon the rest of the day in quiet retirement. His wife joined their daughter and grandson at their daughter's church for an evening service.

On their way to the church service, Maroon's daughter told his wife, "He was talking to himself again while he rested on a bench as we toured the ship. He didn't even see us waving to him, he was so engrossed in his imaginary audience."

Maroon's wife pursed her lips, shrugged, and shook her head. Maroon's grandson in the car seat in the back seat, still recovering from the hike home, decided not to correct his mother.

Maroon, meanwhile, was free for the evening to nurse his tired frame with his feet up in his office, rehydrating with iced tea. He was also free to process his encounter with O'Malley.

Maroon had liked O'Malley. He learned from some simple research at his desk that Raymond O'Malley was an ordinary seaman, not an officer or other person of special authority or note. Extraordinarily, he had lived for another sixty-four years after the *Escanaba*'s 1943 sinking, to the ripe old age of 86. The other lone survivor, seaman Melvin Baldwin, died just twenty years after the incident, leaving O'Malley alone to commemorate his departed shipmates at Grand Haven's annual Coast Guard event.

O'Malley's legacy became much more than his miraculous rescue. No, he didn't earn any fortune with which to build and bless Grand Haven. But O'Malley's singular contribution may have been every bit as great as the men and women who did earn fortunes to seed back into the community's rich soil. O'Malley returned every summer to the Coast Guard festival to honor his departed shipmates. That's it. He made the trek.

O'Malley's insistence on traveling to Grand Haven every summer to light a candle in honor of his shipmates' ultimate sacrifice, right up to his last attendance in a wheelchair, multiplied the impact of the annual ceremony. Without many words and with hardly any actions, O'Malley made a simple but profound contribution to Grand Haven's special culture. O'Malley proved that community requires sacrifice. The greater the sacrifice, the greater the community.

As the evening cooled, Maroon decided to sit on the deck behind his residence, overlooking the cemetery to the west. The sun had fallen in the sky enough to cast a softer light across the cemetery's rolling expanse, against the dramatic backdrop of the tall, wooded dunes. The view of the undulating bright expanse curtained with towering forest was one that Maroon treasured in all seasons, light, and weather. But he especially appreciated the view when the evening light glinted across it, highlighting whatever mist, humidity, pollen, insects, or birds floated across it in the light evening breeze.

Sitting on the back deck in the precious peace of the evening, Maroon considered how the figures he had encountered, and so many other people about whom he knew and whom he didn't know, had each sacrificed to make Grand Haven what it is.

In his view across the cemetery, Maroon could just make out the Civil War memorial, a raised platform with concrete walls and tall statue of a soldier standing with his musket. The platform held a couple dozen graves of Grand Haven soldiers who served in the Civil War. Nearby, also within Maroon's view, another plot, flying the nation's flag, honored Grand Haven soldiers who had died in other conflicts. The American Legion held annual Memorial Day events at the plot, complete with 21-gun salute.

Many Grand Haven residents had given their lives to protect their community. Maroon had a peculiar connection to one of them.

Scott Flahive was a young Grand Haven police officer when in 1994 a jail break occurred. The county's old jail was right downtown, hard by Grand Haven's old courthouse. Accomplices picked up one of the escapees in a waiting vehicle but got no farther than the city's main drag, where officers blocked the vehicle.

Officer Flahive was the first to approach the vehicle to apprehend the suspects before they could wreak further harm and havoc. The prisoners had already brutally beaten a female guard with a laundry bag filled with chunks of concrete. The accomplices within the vehicle, though, had armed one of the escapees with a rifle with which the escapee shot and killed Flahive as he approached. Flahive lost his life to save others. A jury convicted the escapee of Flahive's murder.

When a police officer dies in the line of duty, other officers come out to honor the sacrifice. For Flahive's memorial, hundreds of police vehicles from across the state followed the hearse to the grand cemetery behind Maroon's residence. Wanting to do his own small part to honor the fallen officer, Maroon hiked through the cemetery and woods to stand in a solitary spot along the road into the cemetery. Hundreds of other residents had taken up other spots along the memorial parade route to honor Flahive's sacrifice, but Maroon stood alone at the edge of the woods, watching the police vehicles roll slowly by, losing count of their enormous number.

The solemn parade moved Maroon deeply, as it moved so many other residents. By the time Maroon caught sight of the hearse, he knew he needed to do more than simply stare as it rolled by. Other onlookers had clapped, bowed their heads in prayer, or saluted. Maroon, though, felt compelled to kneel in the slushy snow at his feet in honor of the fallen officer and prayer for his grieving family members. The hearse rolled past. Maroon rose again to his feet, pants soaked from the slushy snow, to hike back to his residence.

Maroon later read a news account of the memorial parade and service in which a family member of the fallen officer acknowledged having been moved by the lone figure kneeling in the snow along the road into the cemetery. Maroon's tiny act of sacrifice, one he assumed to be inconsequential and unknown to anyone but him, had made its own small contribution to Grand Haven's fabric of care, honor, civic duty, and communion.

As he sat on his back deck in the evening's peace, Maroon's thoughts soon turned to other sacrifices many made, investing their large or small fortunes, their great or modest talents, or simply their time and trouble, to weave and sustain the community's rich tapestry. Maroon recalled his father-in-law attending countless hospital, rotary, Coast Guard festival, church, and other board and committee meetings, to keep the community's charitable services and civic spirit alive.

The seaman O'Malley had sacrificed in service. But so, too, had the others whom Maroon had encountered, including Ferry, Robinson, River Woman, Mr. and Mrs. Duncan, Miss White, Cutler, Loutit, Mr. and Mrs. Saunders, and Akeley. Countless and nameless others had also sacrificed to sustain and promote the Grand Haven community. Those who simply went honestly to work in the city's fields, woods, factories, shops, and offices each day were sacrificing their time and energies to foster and sustain a sound community. Without sacrifice, Grand Haven would not have been a community. Without sacrifice, Grand Haven would not have existed.

Without sacrifice, families would not exist, either, as the foundation for community. Maroon knew well the sacrifices his wife and daughter made for his family and for others. He knew, too, how other families sacrificed for their members and for the community, as the community's foundation. The greater the willingness of family members to sacrifice in devotion and care for one another, the greater the community.

The seaman O'Malley, though, had left Maroon with another thought. What had O'Malley said, something about *getting the right grip*?

Maroon had understood immediately what O'Malley meant by holding tight to loved ones. Maroon wanted his wife, daughter, and grandson to know that they had his love, care, service, protection, and support. He would hold fast to them through thick and thin, God willing.

Yet Maroon also understood what O'Malley meant by not holding too tight. Maroon and his daughter could stifle the growth and development of Maroon's grandson, for instance, if they protected, limited, constrained, and restricted him too much. Relationships of all kinds, including not just parent and child, husband and wife, and brother and sister, but also friend to friend and coworker to coworker, depend on a grip neither too tight nor too loose.

As Maroon reflected over O'Malley's insight, he recalled the odd fact he had learned recently about the correlation between the strength of one's physical handgrip and the strength of one's mental grasp of the meaning of things. Evidently, as children grow in their physical grip strength, they simultaneously grow in their cognitive grasp. Likewise, as the elderly decline in their grip strength, they simultaneously decline in their mental acuity. The correlation apparently extends to the injury or illness of individuals of all ages, where a weakened physical grip generally means a weakened cognitive grasp.

Maroon understood that correlation does not necessarily mean causation. Cognition may rise or fall in the young, elderly, and individuals of all other ages, coincidentally rather than causally with physical grip strength. But Maroon believed that the relationship might have more to it than coincidence. After all, when we speak of *getting a grip on things*, we naturally analogize physical and mental grip. But it's not just semantics. Even more to the point, we reason in order to physically grasp. And we physically grasp in order to further our purpose in reasoning.

Maroon's musing over getting the proper grip led him back to his own quandary. Sitting on the porch, watching the sun fall lower in the sky to provide a progressively more dramatic backlighting to his beautiful cemetery view, Maroon began to consider again how he was to proceed in navigating these otherworldly encounters. His momentary abandonment of caution at Escanaba Park that afternoon, when he briefly no longer hid his encounter with O'Malley from the watchful eye of his daughter, was a concerning new sign. Maroon sensed that he was getting in deeper and deeper.

Just then, a figure moving through the cemetery caught Maroon's eye. People strolled along the cemetery's narrow asphalt roads all the time. But this figure had come straight over one of the rolling green dunes, as if out of the woods. The figure, a tall female moving elegantly across the dune, headed in a straight line without respect to path or topography, in the way that Maroon had seen fox glide across the cemetery on their singular path, unmoved by the ordinary routes of others.

Maroon watched from his seat on the deck as the figure headed straight toward Maroon's residence, up and down across the rolling dune. Soon, the tall woman, in Native American dress, reached the corner of Maroon's lot. Seeing Maroon, who now stood on his deck to watch her progress, the woman stopped to give Maroon a solemn nod of her head in acknowledgment. Maroon nodded back, knowing full well that her appearance was his next celestial encounter. Figures in ancient native dress just don't walk out of the woods in solemn greeting.

"Care to join me?" Maroon invited the woman, with a wave of his hand toward the chairs on his deck.

Maroon instantly regretted the invitation, suspecting that it might have sounded too forward and, worse, might soon lead to further complications. But the woman had already nodded her acceptance and resumed her way toward Maroon's deck. In another moment, she was mounting the steps to take the seat that Maroon offered her. Maroon sat next to her, the two of them looking back out over the cemetery.

"I know these encounters have been troubling," the woman said without greeting or other formality, instead getting right to the point.

Maroon, though, felt he needed an introduction, just to get some grasp on this next otherworldly event. He inquired, as respectfully as he could, "Might I have the privilege of an introduction?"

"Magdelaine LaFramboise," she replied bluntly, adding for context, "You've already discerned my connection with your prior guests Mr. Robinson and his wife."

Indeed, the moment Madame LaFramboise shared her name, Maroon recalled from his research on Rix Robinson and his wife River Woman that they had acquired an upriver trading post from the half-French and half-Indian woman now seated next to Maroon.

Maroon realized later that Madame LaFramboise might be the earliest Grand Haven resident whose identity we know. Her father Jean Baptiste Marcot, born in the early 1700s, was a French agent for a fur company. Marcot married a younger Ottawa tribe member Marie Nekesh, with whom Marcot had seven children. Madame LaFramboise was the youngest of those children.

Natives killed Marcot when Madame LaFramboise was just two years old, leaving her mother to raise her children in a volatile mix of conflicting and even warring French, English, and Native American cultures. The fatherless family ended up at the mission on Mackinac Island, where Madame LaFramboise accepted baptism and received an education at the mission school, refining her knowledge of French, English, and several native languages.

Madame LaFramboise's mother moved the family to the Grand River's mouth, nearly half a century before Reverend Ferry landed there to establish Grand Haven as a settlement on the site of Robinson's remote trading post. Madame LaFramboise, the figure seated next to Maroon on his deck, grew to maturity in Grand Haven, when it was a village of the Lac Courtes Oreilles tribe. As a teenager and young woman, Madame LaFramboise walked the very dunes over which she and Maroon looked from the deck of his residence.

Madame LaFramboise married her husband Joseph LaFramboise in 1794. Together, they developed the fur trade along the lower Grand River. Each fall, they would bring their trade goods down from Mackinac Island to their Grand River trading posts. Each spring, they would return to Mackinac Island with the furs for which they had traded. But just as natives had killed Madame LaFramboise's French father, a native also murdered her French husband, leaving the widow to operate their trading posts alone. She did so with great profit, enough to build her fine retirement home back on Mackinac Island after selling her last trading post to Robinson.

"I'm not here to complicate matters further for you but instead to console and encourage you," Madame LaFramboise shared with Maroon.

Maroon sensed the urgency of her admission. He, too, was concerned that his wife would soon return home, producing the very complication both Maroon and Madame LaFramboise hoped to avoid.

"My message is that you integrate your worlds in the way that I integrated mine," Madame LaFramboise continued.

Maroon understood what she meant. From the moment he had first learned of Madame LaFramboise's extraordinary life, he had marveled at her ability to bridge distinct worlds. Maroon had felt the same way about Robinson's wife River Woman and, indeed, about Robinson himself. Even Reverend Ferry had been a master at bridging worlds.

Realizing that he could barely conceive of accomplishing the seemingly impossible task of effectively navigating two such distinct worlds, Maroon turned to Madame LaFramboise seated beside him, asking simply, "How?"

"Every life involves integration of disparate parts," she promptly replied in an almost expressionless demeanor.

After letting her words land and come to rest wherever they might in Maroon's soul, Madame LaFramboise added, once again without expression, "We each choose which of an infinite number of ancestors, experiences, events, attributes, pursuits, and commitments to honor. You must open your heart, mind, and ways to the best of them."

Maroon opened his mouth to share another question in reply, but the sound of his wife's greeting coming from behind him interrupted him. Maroon turned to see his wife standing in the doorway to the deck behind him.

Madame LaFramboise likewise turned to regard Maroon's wife. With her first hint of a softened expression, Madame LaFramboise remarked kindly to Maroon, "She's a lovely woman. You're fortunate to share your lives together."

12

Maroon rose quickly to greet his wife, saying, "Sorry, Honey. I didn't hear you come in."

"What are you doing back here?" she asked in reply.

Maroon detected a note of suspicion in his wife's voice, instantly raising his heartbeat beyond where it had already leapt.

"Just ... enjoying the sunset," Maroon stammered in reply.

Out of the corner of his eye, Maroon caught Madame LaFramboise smiling warmly as she looked back and forth between Maroon and his wife, following their conversation.

"Want to join me?" Maroon asked his wife.

No sooner had the words left his mouth, than Maroon realized his error. He should have abandoned the deck for the relative safety of the house, where Madame LaFramboise might leave Maroon and his wife so that they could sort things out for the late remainder of the evening.

"Sure, for a few minutes," Maroon's wife replied to his dismay.

Maroon watched in horror as his wife moved in the direction of the seat where Madame LaFramboise still sat. But Maroon need not have worried. Anticipating the complication, Madame LaFramboise was already rising to vacate the seat for Maroon's wife.

Maroon thought that Madame LaFramboise might depart, in whatever fashion suited her otherworldly nature and disposition. But instead, she stepped aside to let Maroon's wife sit. The great madame then remained standing comfortably aside with an amused look, apparently ready to observe Maroon's domestic conversation.

Her look irritated Maroon. But Madame LaFramboise promptly indicated her intention to do more than simply observe.

"Remember, friend," she intoned to Maroon, "Integrate your worlds with the best of both of them."

Maroon glanced at Madame LaFramboise, less in acknowledgment than in warning or even chastisement. He wasn't in the mood for coaching. He had his wife with whom to reckon. He had hoped to retire peacefully after another bigger-than-warranted day.

"Aren't you going to sit?" Maroon's wife asked.

Maroon almost jumped but otherwise managed with reasonable equanimity to return to the seat he had just vacated to greet his wife.

"How was your evening?" she asked.

"Fine," Maroon replied guardedly. Having no desire to talk about himself, he quickly asked, "How was the sermon?"

The next few minutes passed in relative tranquility, although Maroon sensed that his wife knew that something was up. Something *was* up. Madame LaFramboise continued to quietly coach Maroon through their conversation, saying kind things about his wife while suggesting diplomatic responses and fruitful lines of inquiry.

Maroon's irritation at the great madame's presumption gradually dissipated. Her observations were consoling. Her suggestions were so apt, as Maroon learned to accept and pursue them, that Maroon was soon glad for her persistence on the scene.

"Well, I'm bushed," Maroon's wife finally admitted, rising to head to bed.

"Me, too," Maroon replied, rising with her.

Yet no sooner had Maroon stood up, than he realized that he would be unceremoniously abandoning the gracious Madame LaFramboise. So, halfway in the door, Maroon called after his wife, saying, "I'll be down in a few minutes."

Maroon listened for any objection. Hearing none, he eased back onto the deck, slowly closing the door behind him while making sure that it made no sound. Looking at Madame LaFramboise, Maroon tipped his head in the direction of the steps off the deck, silently inviting her to follow him around the corner of the house. Once around the corner of the house, Maroon addressed her in an urgent whisper.

"Thank you for the help," Maroon said, preparing to politely encourage her departure.

"No need for thanks," Madame LaFramboise said easily in a normal voice, "We've been the ones disturbing you."

"No, no," Maroon whispered back, "You've been no disturbance. I mean, I'm deeply indebted and very glad for the visits. It's just...."

Maroon's voice trailed off, allowing Madame LaFramboise to finish his whispered sentence, saying, "...complicated."

"Exactly," Maroon whispered back. Once again ready to urge his guest's departure, he added, "Well, I've got to get back. I'm... expected, you know?"

"Oh, I know," Madame LaFramboise said with a good chuckle, while pointing over Maroon's shoulder.

Maroon's face fell aghast.

"You are an odd bird," the voice of Maroon's wife called to him pleasantly from behind, before Maroon could even turn to look.

Maroon slowly turned to see his wife, dressed in her nightgown and robe, hands on her hips in defiance but wearing a pitying smile on her face. She had come out the front door of the house and circled around to see what was up with her missing husband.

"I presume you'll be in soon?" she asked in mock admonishment, its severity relieved by her amused smile.

Maroon nodded sheepishly in reply. When his wife disappeared back around the front of the house, Maroon turned back to bid Madame LaFramboise off. But she had already gone. Maroon just thought he caught a glimpse of her gliding far off across the rolling cemetery, like a fox on its straight-line hunt.

Maroon slept soundly that night, without nightmares or even dreams. He realized after he woke that it had been the first night of reasonable rest, without lurid visions stirring his mind during sleep. The thought occurred to him that his gradual embrace, during waking hours, of the realm beyond might be relieving his mind of its equivalent night's work. A day acknowledging the divine might bring a night with no need of dealing with its demons.

Maroon was tremendously grateful for his wife's grace, shown late the prior evening, over his appearing to be talking to himself. He hoped that his daughter might soon share an equivalent mercy. Perhaps the two would confer and come to that understanding. He suspected that they may well have already done so. He had often felt as if he was a subject of their frequent discourse, which he generally didn't mind, given their common propensity to overlook his many faults.

To demonstrate his appreciation, Maroon redoubled his typical efforts to show his wife his own common favor. Throughout the morning, he rose to chores when she rose to chores. He sat for rest when she sat for rest. By the late morning, chores had mostly been defeated or at least chastened severely. Maroon and his wife sat in the shade of their summer umbrella in the front of the house, with no other agenda than to keep one another's company.

Soon, the familiar sound of a parachute opening high in the sky above caught their attention. They looked at one another and then peered into the sky around the umbrella's edge.

"There they are," Maroon's wife pointed into the sky in the southeast direction.

Maroon nodded, replying, "Looks like three of them."

Grand Haven maintains a small airport for private planes. An enterprising local aviator had for some years been offering skydiving services, including tandem jumps for the complete novice, jumping lessons for students, and unguided jumps for experienced skydivers. Residents could often see the jumpers' bright parachutes floating lazily down in wide circles, to land back at the airport.

On some days, Maroon and his wife could also hear the ripping sound of the parachutes as they opened. On rare days, one could also hear the excited shrieks of the skydivers, presumably the novices, as the chutes opened. And once in a blue moon, one could hear the skydivers' voices, talking back and forth to one another in their slowly descending, lazy circles.

Maroon watched as the skydivers disappeared from sight. When he let his gaze return from the sky, though, Maroon was startled to see a figure sitting comfortably under the umbrella with Maroon and his wife. The figure wore an aviator's clothing, as the attire suitable for piloting appeared in the early days of flight. Maroon's wife was, of course, oblivious to the aviator's otherworldly appearance.

"Quite a sight, isn't it?" the aviator asked Maroon.

Maroon's eyes widened in instinctive response to the eerie stimulus of the aviator's sudden appearance. Maroon did his best to hide it. The morning had gone so well after the prior evening's complications brought by Madame LaFramboise's visit, that Maroon didn't want to disturb things. He let his eyes fall and wander naturally, trying hard not to look directly at the aviator.

"That's alright," the aviator reassured Maroon, "I understand the situation. I just thought I'd drop in for a visit."

The aviator paused to laugh at his unintentional pun. He had indeed dropped in, much like the skydivers. Maroon stifled the roll of his eyes that he wanted to share, over the aviator's self-amusement.

"You can look me up later," the aviator continued, once he had recovered sufficiently from his burst of self-induced amusement, "But I'm James Mars, born right here in Grand Haven in 1875."

Maroon did research Mars in a quiet moment later that afternoon, confirming that the aviation pioneer Mars was born to Captain Thomas McBride and Mary Frances Fallon in Grand Haven in that very year. Mars had changed his McBride name, presumably to aid his peculiar career as an aviation figure and air show and circus entertainer.

That Mars was born into the McBride home made sense, Maroon figured as he learned the little bit of family history he could discover. Captain McBride piloted barges from Grand Haven, across the lake to Milwaukee, and down the lake to Chicago. Of the three regions Captain McBride's barges served, the McBrides chose for their residence the smaller and, to its residents, far more peaceful and beautiful Grand Haven.

Unfortunately, Grand Haven didn't hold quite enough charm to keep Captain McBride's domestic attention. Newspaper accounts of the day indicate that when young Mars née McBride was just eight years old, his father abandoned his barge in Chicago and disappeared with $500 in his pocket. Although initially reported as dead when Chicago authorities found a body in the water, later reports placed him in San Francisco with only $5 remaining of his funds. McBride had exhausted a relative fortune in a few short days of mysterious travel.

The same reports shared and credited Captain McBride's account that on the day of his disappearance, he had smoked an intoxicating cigar in a Chicago shop, only to awaken in San Francisco. He wasn't dead, although he might soon be. At the least, Captain McBride faced further and more-plausible and convincing explanation upon his return to Grand Haven, where his wife was caring for the young Mars and his younger sister, while also pregnant.

Mars inherited his barge-captain father's itch for travel and transportation, but not of the water-borne type. Mars grew to maturity just as the fledgling aviation industry was taking flight. Upon his emancipation, Mars first attached himself to the famous hot-air balloonist Thomas Scott Baldwin, whom history credits as the first American to descend from a balloon by parachute. Under Baldwin's tutelage, Mars likewise became a noted balloonist. Mars was just sixteen years old when he, like his mentor Baldwin, jumped from a balloon to land safely by parachute.

As flight moved from balloons or dirigibles to airplanes, Mars made himself a student of Glenn Curtiss, the aviation engine manufacturer and celebrated founder of the American aviation industry. Mars barnstormed with Curtiss at air shows across the country in the early 1900s. Mars soon extended his performing itinerary around the world, making early or even first flights in Hawaii, Japan, the Philippines, and Korea. At his death long later in 1944, Mars' *New York Times* obituary credited him with giving Japan's Emperor Hirohito his first plane flight.

Maroon could tell that Mars had a very different spirit from the other extraordinary figures whom Maroon had countenanced over the past several days. Mars was a daredevil, a circus entertainer, and very much a bird of amusement and flight. Some reports hint that he eventually became an airport operator and may have developed interests in real estate. But by all other reports, neither Grand Haven nor any other location could hold him.

Maroon thus found it fitting to discover in his research that afternoon that Mars had died in 1944 at age 68, not in Grand Haven but in Los Angeles. Mars could have joined other celebrated Grand Haven figures in burial in the cemetery behind Maroon's residence. But that resting place would not have fit Mars' character. That Los Angeles National Cemetery instead holds Mars' earthly remains fits his character perfectly. Los Angeles is the place itching American original spirits go, to look even further west across the waters from which their dreams and destinies call them.

Mars, though, had anticipated Maroon's very thoughts on this subject, as the other divine figures had similarly read Maroon's mind.

"My father's free spirit must have affected me more than I knew when I was a boy growing up in Grand Haven,"

Mars observed wistfully, as he relaxed in his seat under the shade of the umbrella.

Maroon glanced at his wife, who fiddled with her phone, still oblivious to Mars' presence and observations.

"I'd guess that my aviation endeavors and related world travels were, in a way, a search for my father or perhaps for my own home," Mars continued. He added, "Funny that my search took me aloft, in celestial pursuit of what I hadn't found in a very lovely but earthbound, and by my father abandoned, Grand Haven."

Maroon wanted to look appreciatively at Mars for the very deeply personal insights Mars was sharing. But Maroon resisted the temptation, except for a sly little wink or twitch of the corner of his eye that Maroon granted his celestial guest. Mars caught Maroon's acknowledgement with a smile.

"Yes, you surely understand," Mars said, adding, "For your restless childhood, not entirely unlike my own, led you to adopt your wife's deep roots in Grand Haven."

Mars' generous observation had precisely pegged Maroon's own history and thoughts. As a child, Maroon had necessarily followed the dreams that his father and mother pursued south, west, and points in between, across the American landscape. Maroon's parents, like Mars, eventually landed in Southern California. Maroon, though, had jumped ship as soon as he reached maturity in Michigan, where he met his wife, a Grand Haven native. They soon made Grand Haven their permanent and happy home.

"I don't regret my barnstorming," Mars shared. After a moment's pause with a glance toward Maroon's wife, Mars added, "Although I do regret not having found a home in which to love a wife and children, raising a sound and happy family."

Mars paused again before adding with a sly smile at Maroon, "I suppose you'd want to ask me if I had any advice or message for you."

Maroon twitched the corner of his eye, intending an affirmative response. His wife glanced at him, asking, "Is your eye alright? Seems like it's bothering you."

"Probably allergies," Maroon replied in half or quarter truth. Maroon's eyes had indeed been itching, although that had not been the cause for Maroon's effort at an affirmative signal.

Mars laughed, saying, "Well played, my boy. You're getting the hang of things after all. Maybe you can navigate two worlds without losing any good part of either one of them."

Maroon couldn't resist a small smile in response. Mars was evidently well aware of the wisdom Maroon had been receiving in his prior celestial encounters.

"Something funny?" Maroon's wife asked, having caught her husband's inexplicable smile.

"Just thinking of our good times here together," Maroon replied in another half truth. He had been reacting to Mars' observation, but that observation had indeed reminded him how good his earthly life had been in sacred union with his wife.

"Awww," Maroon's wife replied, reaching over to lay her hand over Maroon's hand, "That's so sweet."

Maroon smiled at her. Mars had another good laugh.

"Now you've got it," Mars enjoined Maroon in the midst of his amusement, "Let one world feed the other."

Mars looked out from under the umbrella, up into the sky.

"You know, I'd best be going," Mars observed to Maroon, adding, "I hear the call of the sky. Glad to see that you're improving. We were worried about you."

Maroon resisted the temptation to bid Mars a fitting goodbye. Instead, with Mars still seated beside them, Maroon suggested to his wife, "Getting a little warm?"

Maroon's wife nodded, replying, "I've had enough."

Husband and wife rose to retire to the cool of the house, while Mars calmly watched them depart. When, moments later, Maroon snuck a glance back outside, Mars was gone.

13

That day and its prior evening proved a watershed for Maroon in his managing the affairs of his two realms, the one in which he lived with great familiarity if not a little stress and the one to which he looked forward but from which he was already receiving regular visitations. Maroon had reached a certain level of tolerance if not outright comfort with the otherworldly goings on. For the first time, he could imagine that they might continue without completely upending his earthly life.

Maroon felt enormous relief over having had the guidance of Madame LaFramboise and the consolation of Mars in the prior twenty-four hours, in his wife's presence but without her undue disturbance. Yet as much relief as Maroon felt, he also began to wonder about the broader import of his increasingly familiar visitations from the great beyond. For the first time, Maroon wondered if he was dying.

Maroon wasn't a hypochondriac. He didn't foresee his impending demise in every little ache or pain. He had a reasonably high tolerance for disease and disability. Like most individuals, Maroon had successfully persevered his way through his fair share of them. He generally believed that his final demise wasn't near, although he also knew that it could come at any time. Yet his visits from beyond were slowly changing his mind. He sensed that they were preparing him for his step across the great threshold into the beyond.

Accordingly, Maroon took stock of his physical health. He had already given plenty of attention to his mental health in the course of navigating his celestial visits. But Maroon was under the impression that his earthly demise would require a physical collapse, of which he expected that sooner or later he would see some sign.

Maroon knew that the events of recent days had taxed not only his mental and emotional condition but also his physical reserves. He had gradually become increasingly exhausted. In his relatively advanced age, he had long ago lost the natural vitality of youth. When something came up, he now had to assess his ability and readiness to handle it rather than simply jumping in with the excess of reserves that youth offers. Yet he was generally up to whatever his tasks demanded or recreations offered.

But in the few prior days, Maroon found himself not up to much of anything without a greater-than-usual struggle. He had, for instance, hiked to the channel with his daughter and grandson, a significant expenditure of energy under any circumstances. The hike, though, had completely floored him. That's why he had not even considered touring the Coast Guard cutter and had instead languished on the nearest bench. And he hadn't yet really bounced back.

Maroon detected a greater concern, though, than his general exhaustion and failure to recover. Along with his exhaustion, Maroon sensed something going on with his mind or senses. His world was narrowing, whether in his literal vision or figurative view he could not quite tell. But he seemed to have gradually come to the point of living from the reverse end of a telescope or the bottom of a well. He had to concentrate harder than ever simply to focus on what was going on around him, if he hoped to participate in it.

Maroon went to bed that night fully aware of his new concern but resolved to put it aside. It, too, might pass, like the strangeness of his otherworldly encounters. He might soon lose the sense of living his life through a gradually narrowing hallway, regaining his old self. Or he may soon adjust to his newly circumscribed sensory experience of his surroundings, like the blind improving their auditory acuity.

Whatever was to happen next, Maroon decided not to worry about it.

Maroon once again slept soundly, without dreams or nightmares, that night. He woke much later than usual, with no improvement in the declined conditions he had discerned in himself the prior evening. Yet he also woke up looking forward to the probability of another celestial encounter. Remaining in bed for a few more minutes after having awoken, Maroon even surveyed in his mind other famous local figures from whom he had not yet heard, imagining who might appear next.

"Are you up, Honey?" his wife called from somewhere outside the bedroom.

Maroon huffed in minor annoyance at his wife's habit, fortunately rarely necessary, of rousing him out of bed with such a pointed question. If he wasn't up, her call would have made him get up. If he was up already, he wouldn't have needed the call. Maroon chalked up the slight inanity of her question to his wife's grace. Another spouse might have just hollered *get out of bed*!

Maroon stumbled out of the bedroom, greeting his wife who sat at the dining table balancing the checkbook.

"Oh, good," she said, "You're up."

Maroon muttered to himself again over the comment's peculiarity. Of course he was up. She had hollered to him, rousing him out of bed.

"They're going to the hollow," she continued, adding, "They want you to go."

Maroon assumed that his wife meant that his daughter and grandson were going to the playground and ball fields on the other side of the woods in the direction of downtown. Maroon generally loved joining his daughter and grandson on such outings. And he was generally up to it. But this morning, he had no such sense. He was still exhausted, still seeing the world from the wrong end of a telescope.

"When are they leaving?" Maroon asked, to buy time.

"In a few minutes," his wife answered, adding, "You'd better get going."

Apparently, the decision had already been made without his consultation. Yet Maroon would have made the same decision, if it had been his choice. His body often said no to such invitations. But his mind and spirit generally said yes. Indeed, his daughter and grandson were his highest priority, when the question involved allocating limited energy.

Fortunately, the plan was for Maroon to meet them at the hollow, a short drive in his truck away. Maroon easily beat them there, parking in the lot just above the level of the playground and, beyond the playground, the ball field nestled into the base of the soaring dunes.

"That's my favorite ballfield," a gruff voice intoned from beside Maroon.

Maroon gave a small jump in his seat. For there, in the truck seat beside him, sat a big-eared, tough-looking ballplayer in an old flannel uniform.

"Neal Ball," the youthful but nonetheless wizened-looking man said, reaching across the console to offer Maroon his hand, while adding, "Short for Cornelius, if you look me up later. How's that for a ballplayer's name? Maybe I should have been a catcher rather than an infielder and occasional outfielder."

Ball laughed at his own joke, as Maroon took and shook his hand. If the seaman O'Malley's handshake had been ox strong, Ball's handshake was even stronger. Maroon also noticed how rough Ball's skin was and how gnarled his hands, presumably from the rigors of batting without gloves and fielding with only rudimentary hand protection.

Maroon took Ball's garrulity as an excuse to immediately engage him on any mundane subject that came to mind, a departure from Maroon's cautious approach to the prior figures from beyond.

"What did you like about the field?" Maroon asked in response to Ball's casual observation.

"Well, look at it," Ball replied, incredulous at, but appreciative for, Maroon's question. He rambled on, explaining, "Those dunes make one think of Fenway Park with its Green Monster wall, don't they? You know, I played my last season for the Red Sox in Fenway Park, the year after it opened in 1912."

Maroon gawked. He knew Fenway Park was very old, but not that old. And he understood that Ball was a baseball player from the past, but not a *major league* player, and not a player from such a distant and glorious past.

"Sure did," Ball rambled on, "Made the majors in 1907 with the New York Highlanders, then played a couple seasons for the Cleveland Naps before ending up with the Red Sox. Of course, I spent a few years in the minors before then, with the Montgomery Senators of the Southern League. But I was born right here in Grand Haven in 1881."

Maroon smiled at Ball's loquaciousness. The other figures from beyond had mostly been serene, noble, reserved, even regal. Most had chosen their words carefully and spoken with great articulation, which suited Maroon fine in that he was a lawyer and writer. But Maroon loved the rough ease with which Ball spoke. And he knew that ball players, like baseball fans, were often encyclopedic in their knowledge of the sport, happy to share their own stats and awards in instant comparison with the stats and honors of other players.

"Yes, I loved this ball field for its setting," Ball resumed, now speaking wistfully. He continued, "But I also loved it for the weather. You could play here on the hottest day of the summer. You'd swelter at one of the other parks just a mile inland. But here, you'd get a hint of the lake's cool and maybe a nice breeze off the channel waters. And if you didn't find that relief, you could jump in the water later."

Ball paused, basking in the childhood memories. But he soon resumed.

"Hey, you played here yourself, didn't you?" Ball asked Maroon respectfully.

Maroon huffed involuntarily. He was a thirty-year-old lawyer by the time he reached Grand Haven with his wife and their infant daughter. He had indeed played at the sparkling little ball field tucked up against the base of the dune, the field on which they right then gazed. But Maroon's play had been in church leagues with men up to twice his age. And whatever tiny bit of baseball knack Maroon had acquired as an avid fan of the sport when a child and teenager, he had long since lost to disuse and age. He'd had a blast playing, but it was at the lowest possible amateur ranks.

"The way I played baseball here, it might as well have been a different sport entirely," Maroon replied wryly.

"No, no, that's not it at all," Ball replied, "Baseball is baseball. It's a beautiful sport no matter who plays it."

Ball paused, as a vehicle pulled up alongside Maroon's truck.

"Watch," Ball resumed, "Your grandson will play it beautifully, too, and at his age, he can probably barely hit the ball."

Ball tipped his head toward the vehicle that had just pulled up and parked, saying, "That's them now. Let's go have some fun."

Ball was out the truck's door in a flash, with a bounce in his step. As Maroon eased himself out of the truck in pursuit of Ball, Maroon thought he heard Ball whistling gaily.

"Hey, Pa!" Maroon's daughter called to him as he came around the back of the truck to greet her and the little guy.

"Got your ball cap on, don't you," Maroon said to his grandson. Pulling at his own cap, he added, "I've got mine on, too."

"And yours is blue like mine," Maroon's grandson replied proudly.

"Hey," Maroon's daughter chimed in, "You two match shirts and pants, too!"

The little guy looked from his own clothing to Maroon's clothes and back again, smiling. Ball, meanwhile, looked on, slapping his thigh in bawdy amusement. Maroon's daughter was oblivious to Ball's excited presence. Maroon, though, stole a glance at Ball. So did Maroon's grandson. Maroon and his grandson smiled at one another. Maroon winked. His grandson awkwardly tried winking, too. Ball slapped his thigh again in even greater amusement.

"You guys are a riot," Ball said to the two of them.

"Hey, Pa," the little guy said to Maroon, ready to mimic Ball, "We're a riot!"

Maroon's daughter raised her eyebrows and shook her head, saying gaily, "Honey! Where did you learn that?"

The little guy just looked at Maroon, attempting another awkward wink. Ball guffawed so loudly at the little guy's adept byplay that Maroon thought Ball was going to fall down, rolling on the ground.

For his part, Maroon breathed a big sigh of relief. It looked like things were going to be more fun than he expected, as Ball had already surmised. It also astonished and delighted Maroon that his grandson had caught on so quickly to the ruse Maroon must follow to make sense of his two worlds, without embarrassing himself in front of the little guy's mother. Maroon and his grandson were now trusted partners in that ruse, a bond suddenly far deeper than any a grandparent had a right to expect. The celestial encounters had brought Maroon yet another inestimable gift of a closer bond with his grandson.

Maroon, his daughter, and his grandson whiled away the next two hours at various forms of play, a little of it involving baseball, a lot of it just meandering about, trying out playground apparatus or just climbing up and rolling down the dune.

Out of respect for Ball's presence, Maroon soon coaxed his grandson into trying his little hand at baseball. Maroon had brought along a couple of adult fielding gloves and an adult ball and bat. Ball watched in hilarious enjoyment as Maroon's grandson tried without success to wear the huge glove or wield the huge bat.

The little guy could throw the ball and catch it a little bit, having already played a lot of catch with his Papa. As Maroon caught and tossed the ball with his grandson, Ball watched in fascination, making comments about the little guy's instincts, stance, and methods.

"Oh, he's a lefthander!" Ball regaled Maroon, as the little guy picked up and tossed the ball repeatedly with his left rather than right hand.

"I'm a lefthander, Pa," the little guy repeated, bringing a broad smile from Maroon, guffaws from Ball, and astonishment from Maroon's oblivious daughter.

"Look at how he brings the ball in toward his body as he catches it," Ball noted with appreciation, adding, "He's already learning to move quickly from a catching to a throwing stance."

Taking Ball's cue, the little guy began comically quickening the speed with which he went from catching to throwing. As a consequence, he caught less and when throwing sprayed the ball hither and thither rather than sending it reliably toward Maroon.

"I'm going from catching to throwing quicker, Pa," the little guy explained, repeating Ball's observation, to Maroon's amusement, Ball's guffaws, and more astonishment from Maroon's oblivious daughter.

Maroon's daughter soon offered Maroon and her son the little wiffle ball and bat they had brought along. Maroon's grandson accepted the bat, while Maroon stood ready with the ball.

"Oh no," Ball observed, seeing the odd way in which the little guy clutched the bat, "He's a natural cross-hander."

The observation sent Ball off on a ramble about youths he had known who tried without success to persist in the increasingly organized sport, while batting cross-handed. Ball added stories about professional ball players who had amused Ball and themselves by practicing hitting cross-handed, even with a little success.

Ball even shared a brief account of a minor-league teammate of his who, disgusted with the batting slump into which he had fallen, went to the plate for his next at-bat holding the bat cross-handed. The move had not only left both teams, the umpires, and the fans in hilarious amusement but had also made the national sporting press. It had also broken the poor player's slump. According to Ball, he had hit a home run in that very at bat, of course having switched back to the correct grip on the bat.

Meanwhile, in the course of Ball's ramble, Maroon's grandson had, with a bit of Maroon's silent urging, switched his hands to the proper hitting style, no longer cross-handed. With better swings, the little guy actually struck the ball a couple of times, once fairly sharply, as Maroon gently tossed it to him, aiming as best Maroon could for the bat. Maroon's daughter cheered with each strike of the ball.

During a pause in Ball's soliloquy on cross-handed hitters, the little guy observed proudly, "I'm not hitting cross-handed anymore, Pa!"

But the little coaching session was soon over, the little guy bored with the repetition and beginning to feel the weight of the observation and coaching. He dropped the bat to crouch in the grass, examining the carcass of a large beetle. After discovering that it was dead, the little guy rose and headed off toward the dune to sit and roll in the sand.

"Awww, are you all done playing baseball, Honey?" Maroon's daughter asked the little guy, who gave a dismissive wave of his hand without turning back to look at her. He was lost to his imagination.

Maroon looked at Ball with a shrug but then, realizing his error, turned to his daughter to repeat the action.

"Let him go," Ball suggested to Maroon, adding, "Don't force it on him at this age. I've seen too many ball players spoil their children's natural love for the sport."

Maroon started to nod in response but, remembering his daughter, caught himself. When his daughter gave him a glance, he twisted and flexed his neck.

"Did you hurt yourself?" his daughter asked.

"No, I'm fine," Maroon replied, rubbing his neck.

Ball guffawed at Maroon's effort to conceal his surreptitious communication. When Maroon's daughter wasn't looking, Maroon shot Ball a mock scowl, followed by a knowing smile.

Maroon's daughter soon wandered off after her son. Maroon and Ball stood together, watching the pair head for the base of the dune.

"Time for me to go," Ball said to Maroon without removing his gaze from the receding pair.

Maroon nodded, saying a quiet but audible *thanks*, low enough so that his daughter would not hear.

"How about if I leave you with this?" Ball asked. Turning to Maroon, he concluded in a serious and articulate tone that he had not used in his verbose sharing to that point, "Play can be a form of worship, including both a child's free play and an adult's organized competitive sport. It's all about the spirit in which one does it."

Ball clapped Maroon on the shoulder with one of his grizzled hands, while saying, ""Enjoy your grandson, Pardner."

Grand Haven

Maroon turned to watch his daughter and grandson, now sitting on the dune together, digging in the sand. When he turned back to Ball with a smile, Ball was gone.

14

Maroon sat alone in his office late that morning, relishing the time he'd shared not only with his daughter and grandson but also with Ball. To Maroon, Ball's easy jocularity represented the best spirit of baseball, bringing back to mind the best times Maroon had playing the sport. Ball obviously took the sport seriously. He must have done so, to have reached the major leagues. But Ball had found a way of preserving the sport's joy, even while respecting its demanding requirements.

Maroon wondered what role the little field tucked into the base of the dune had played in both Ball's joy in the game and Ball's dedication to it. Maroon also wondered what father, grandfather, brother, coach, or other person had fostered that joy and dedication in Ball. Maroon regretted that he had not had the occasion to ask Ball and hear Ball's rambling answer.

Yet while Maroon turned the morning's events over in his mind with delicious pleasure, he also grew increasingly concerned about his condition, which the morning's effort appeared to have worsened. His tunnel vision had grown more severe, he was certain. He squinted across the office and out the windows toward the cemetery, alarmed at how the view was narrowing and receding. Maroon's body didn't feel any better. Indeed, he felt a slight but constant quivering.

For a moment, Maroon thought of getting up from his desk to go tell his wife. But he knew that she'd insist he go to the hospital and that when he refused, she would schedule an appointment with his doctor. And he wasn't ready for that fuss. He resolved instead to let the day pass in rest. Perhaps if he occupied his mind with other things, he would notice later that his condition had improved.

Maroon summoned the energy to turn to his pending writing assignments. After a couple of hours of concentrated effort, Maroon felt better, not mentally or physically but in having retained his essential faculties despite his declining condition. Maroon had long treated his illnesses and disabilities with little demonstrations of capacity, making him feel alive if not healed and better. He was sure his method wasn't what the doctor ordered. Rest probably would have been better. But belief in one's persistent capability is sometimes a better tonic than rest or medication.

In midafternoon, Maroon decided to go get an iced tea at the local diner. His wife declined his invitation to join him, having already made arrangements to visit with a friend down the street. They would go together later. Maroon climbed slowly into his truck. He sat in the truck in the garage for a minute before heading out, just to be sure that he was even up to driving. But within a few minutes, he had navigated to the diner, acquired his tea, and returned to the truck for his short drive home.

Maroon pulled up to the corner where he would turn home rather than toward downtown. Feeling the need for a little longer diversion, Maroon turned toward downtown instead of home. A few blocks later, he was downtown, with no errand or other reason. Not wanting to drive aimlessly around, he pulled into the mostly empty parking lot of the enormous County Courthouse. Rolling down the truck's windows for some fresh air, Maroon turned the truck off, to sip at his tea and gaze at the mammoth Courthouse.

"Quite a sight, isn't it?" a voice intoned from beside him.

This time, Maroon didn't jump, as he had jumped that morning at the unexpected voice of Neal Ball. Maroon instead looked calmly over to assess the small but imposing figure seated comfortably in the truck's passenger seat. He was dressed in what would pass today for a tuxedo or formal wear, although of an antiquated sort. Maroon recognized the clothing as judicial dress of a much earlier day. Maroon had half expected it, given that the two of them sat gazing up at the grand Courthouse.

"Good afternoon, Your Honor," Maroon greeted the figure with the address Maroon had used a thousand times before in the courtroom.

"Good afternoon, Counselor," the imposing figure replied without a hint of familiarity, instead austerely, as appellate judges generally spoke from the bench.

An awkward pause followed. Maroon took the cue, saying, "I'm Maroon, appearing for the defense on a motion to withdraw."

On the spur of the moment, Maroon couldn't think of anything else. But his quick courtroom wit had done the trick.

"Ah," the distinguished jurist observed in response while sharing his first smile, "You're moving to withdraw, are you? That's not going to be easy in my court."

Maroon chuckled, replying, "No, Your Honor, I wouldn't expect so. It's my first-ever motion to withdraw."

The distinguished jurist laughed in response. They had broken the ice for a good conversation, while recognizing the great jurist's distinction.

It is true that motions to withdraw generally draw the ire of a trial judge. Trial judges don't want a hapless party left without a lawyer, to muck up basic court procedures and clog the court's docket. It was also true that Maroon had never attempted to withdraw from a case. Like most other lawyers, he routinely stuck with a case through thick or thin to the bitter end, even when a case went badly awry, which happens to most lawyers if not all, and even when a client refused to cooperate. Some clients are their own worst enemy.

Maroon, though, still didn't know his visitor's identity, even if he had discerned his visitor's judicial role. Another awkward pause ensued, finally broken by the jurist.

"Epaphroditus Ransom," he said, extending a hand across the truck for Maroon to shake. He added, "I was the county's first circuit judge, from 1836 to 1838, if I recall correctly. It was a shorter term. The governor wanted me on the state's high court."

Maroon raised his eyebrows in surprise, while nodding. He hadn't known or had forgotten that the county's first judge received swift elevation to the state's supreme court. It seemed a strange thing that a circuit-riding judge from mostly unsettled West Michigan would get the governor's nod for the state's high court. But politics makes for strange bedfellows.

The exquisitely named Epaphroditus Ransom was born in Massachusetts around 1798, with some disagreement over both the year and the date. The original *Epaphroditus* was a New Testament figure associated with the city of Philippi and both a Catholic and Eastern Orthodox saint, giving hints of the affinities of Ransom's parents. Imagine naming the courage and clarity it took to name a newborn *Epaphroditus*.

Epaphroditus Ransom earned his law degree in 1823 in Massachusetts but opened his first law practice nearby in Vermont. He married there, having four children, two of whom died in infancy. Ransom also won election to Vermont's state house. But when several of his many siblings moved to Michigan Territory, Ransom decided to join them, giving up his successful Vermont law practice and legislative career in 1834 for the rigors of settling, farming, and starting a new law practice in the western territory.

Ransom and his family settled well south of Grand Haven. Ransom had little direct connection with Grand

Haven, other than his appointment as Ottawa County's first judge. Grand Haven is the County seat, where the main courthouse has long been located. But when Ransom received his judicial appointment, earned from his connections in the Michigan legislature to which his fellow citizens had elected him, Ransom was a circuit-riding judge. He rode horseback through the wilderness from site to site in the County, wherever the litigants could conveniently gather, accompanied by the party's circuit-riding lawyers. Judging in wild territory differs from judging in a settled society.

Yet Ransom was still Grand Haven's first official judge. And he may well have ridden horseback into the nascent settlement to decide disputes, as he rode horseback into other lakeshore communities.

In any case, Ransom's circuit riding was short lived. The governor appointed him to the new state's supreme court, where Ransom served for a decade beginning in 1838. For the last half of that decade, Ransom was the supreme court's chief justice, proving once again his swift rise to leadership. And Ransom wasn't just about leading. He was also about doing justice. His noted 1840 ruling prevented state removal of Potawatomi tribes from their Southwest Michigan lands.

By 1848, Ransom was Michigan's governor, the first to serve in the new state capitol Lansing. But his governorship was short lived when his Democratic Party refused to renominate him for governor in the 1850 election because of Ransom's anti-slavery position.

Ransom returned to the state legislature in subsequent years, where his broad influence continued. As the first president of the Michigan Agricultural Society, Ransom helped start Michigan State University, then the Agricultural College of the State of Michigan, a first of its kind in the nation. In a rare span of collegiate loyalties, Ransom also served as a University of Michigan regent. Ransom lived to about age sixty-one, dying in Kansas in 1859 while carrying out an office to which President Ulysses S. Grant had appointed him.

Maroon could tell from the great jurist's reserve that it would be up to Maroon to carry the conversation.

"What do you think of the new courthouse?" Maroon asked, as a conversation starter.

"Big," Ransom answered, adding, "I preferred the original courthouse and didn't even mind the modern one they tore down to build this edifice."

Maroon knew what Ransom meant. The original courthouse to which Ransom referred had an ornate, classical style characteristic of other early Michigan courthouses, several noted nationally for the high quality of their workmanship and style, Grand Haven's courthouse among them. Maroon's wife remembered the old courthouse fondly, from her days as a child riding her bike around the town. That attractive and well-proportioned but antiquated courthouse came down in favor of a modern-looking, green-tile, terrazzo-floor, big-window structure on the same site, which after a few decades of service gave way to the present-day courthouse.

Maroon had practiced in that prior modern courthouse, not this big new one. He had moved on to teaching law by the time the new courthouse opened. He had been in the new courthouse only to sponsor new lawyers for swearing in, meet with judge and lawyer acquaintances, and accompany students on tours. But like Ransom, Maroon's heart wasn't in the big new structure, as well-designed as it was for modern needs.

"You know," Ransom continued, still looking up at the looming structure, "Government is necessary and can even be good. But its place shouldn't be at the pinnacle. I rather preferred when the church steeples in town were the higher structures and the courthouse didn't dwarf the people whom it served."

Indeed, approaching the city along its main highway, one could now see the Courthouse's tower looming over the city, signifying the government's new place at the apex. The city's largest church now lay well outside of town, banished to the margins.

The new Courthouse's planners had built it at the farthest point uphill on the downtown city block where the prior courthouses had stood. The new Courthouse's huge size dwarfed approaching litigants and lawyers in the parking lot below. Moreover, to get into the new Courthouse, visitors had to climb a full two flights of outdoor steps, unless they wanted to hunt for the hidden elevator for disabled access. The Courthouse also limited public access to the double flight of broad steps up from the parking lot, as a security measure.

In short, as handsome as it otherwise looked, and as fitting as it was for the demands of modern justice, the new Courthouse had the feel to Maroon of a fortress, not a community resource. The looming character of the new Courthouse had astonished and disappointed Maroon as the construction finished and the Courthouse opened to the area's residents. He sensed that the great jurist seated next to him might have some of the same sentiments, from the little that the jurist had shared.

"Thank you for your service," Maroon heard himself saying to Ransom, trying to keep their conversation going.

The great jurist didn't seem compelled to speak, satisfied instead to sit in stolid peace in Maroon's truck.

"Well, thank you for your own service," the great jurist replied, glancing at Maroon.

But Ransom continued in his own train of thought, saying, "It was a big move for my young family when we came west to the wilderness of Michigan territory from our well-established home and my law practice and government service in the settled East."

Maroon could hardly imagine the effort that move took and the disruption it caused. He read in his research that night that Ransom's family plodded west for a full month in horse-drawn carts, simply to reach West Michigan. Carving a homestead and farm out of the West Michigan wilds, in the midst of unsettled questions regarding relationships with Native American tribes, must have been a Herculean task, certainly one requiring a strong back and stronger constitution.

"Why did you come West?" Maroon asked, when he saw that the great jurist had no intention of continuing on with his account.

"Good question, Counselor," Ransom observed with another glance across the truck. After a reasonable pause to gather his thoughts, Ransom answered, "Partly to follow others in my family. But that's not the full story."

Once again, the justice stopped short, looking like he had no intention of saying more. But with another polite prompt from Maroon, he soon continued.

"As much as I appreciated the benefits of my law practice and the opportunities of my elected government service back home in Vermont, my wife and I wanted to experience making our own way in a new world. For us, although not for others, the old ways had ossified, even got out of order. We were less a community of equal individuals gathered by consent in the Lord's name than a social system with rigid castes."

Maroon nodded politely, digesting the jurist's exalted thoughts. Maroon even thought for a brief moment that he, too, had come West to Grand Haven with thoughts of making his own way rather than following the set ways of others, within a stratified professional and social class.

But then Ransom turned and smiled at Maroon, adding, "And maybe we just didn't want to be under anyone's thumb, you know?"

Maroon gave an appreciative smile and chuckle. He understood that feeling of the desire for reasonable independence, too. Participation in the community's rituals should be by joyful consent rather than coercion.

"Did you find what you sought?" Maroon asked respectfully.

The justice smiled wryly. While tipping his head this way and that, he answered, "At times yes, at other times no. We shared in some amazing communities, with skilled and dedicated people. And I was glad to be able to pursue my anti-slavery stance, although it cost me greatly. History proved me right on that one. But we also at times consented to or even committed various injustices."

The justice paused, considering his own words, before continuing, "I see great injustices today, too. Do you?"

Maroon dropped his head, nodding.

"Stand for what you know," the great jurist admonished Maroon, repeating, "Stand for what you know."

Ransom paused, gathering his concluding remarks, before adding, "You will make errors, as I did. But be sure you stand for the convictions you know. Respect the contours of your democratic republic, but be sure that you still stand where you know you should."

Maroon nodded again, this time with his head up, peering at Ransom.

"You'd better be going," Ransom said politely, adding, "Will you let me out at Duncan Woods on your way home? I'd like to see a little of my wilderness again."

Maroon smiled and nodded. Starting up the truck and rolling up its windows, he motored off toward home with the great jurist beside him. Reaching the entrance to Duncan Woods, he pulled into its drive to let Ransom out. The justice departed without a look or word back in Maroon's direction, walking not up the paved drive onto which Maroon had pulled the truck but instead off on a tangent, into the deep woods.

As he watched Ransom disappear, Maroon heard an echo deep inside himself to follow the narrow path up to glory, not the broad road down to destruction.

15

Maroon was home within a couple more minutes after dropping Ransom off at the woods. Good thing, because Maroon's brief outing had exhausted him, not refreshed him. Something was up, Maroon was sure. But he still wasn't ready to confront it or to share it with his wife or daughter.

Instead, Maroon went straight to bed, even though it was still afternoon.

"You alright?" Maroon's wife asked, poking her head in the bedroom when back from her visit with her friend down the street.

Maroon nodded, feigning sleepiness while muttering, "Just taking a nap."

In fact, though, Maroon wasn't sleepy. He was sick, not sick with a cold or the flu but instead suffering an even greater narrowing of his vision and other senses, while feeling more exhausted than ever.

Maroon's wife closed the bedroom door quietly behind her, leaving Maroon alone. He was glad to be in bed. At least he could close his eyes to his worrying mental sensations, while staying off his exhausted feet and letting his worn frame rest. Maroon's mind, though, remained at work. He had to think about *something*.

Maroon turned his thoughts to Ransom, thinking of the spectacular fitness of the great jurist's name. Ransom had, like the saint of Philippi for which his parents had named him, made his way out into an unsettled world, carrying a message of hope and liberation. Ransom had sacrificed greatly in doing so, like the Lord, who was his ransom, had sacrificed for him. Hadn't the venerated Christian author C.S. Lewis named the hero of his space trilogy *Ransom*, after the same fashion?

For the first time, Maroon thought of the meaning of his own name. Yes, maroon was a color. But it was the color of a sacrifice, the color of spilled blood, like the blood of the Lord he shared with the great jurist. Ransom and Maroon were of the same stock, not just as lawyer professionals but as humble and wholly inadequate, yet nonetheless dedicated, representatives in the world of that Lord.

Maroon picked up his cell phone from the nightstand beside him, to look up the meaning of his name. Yes, the color of crimson, of blood, but also connoting *deep*, *passionate*, and *rooted*. As Maroon set the cell phone back on the nightstand, he assessed that he didn't think he was any of those things. But he aspired to each of them. And in ways, he had indeed lived out his name, much as Ransom had lived out his unparalleled, magnificent name.

Maroon soon lost his train of thought, his exhaustion finally bringing on merciful sleep.

He awoke to his wife's customary call, "Honey, are you asleep?"

Well, no, not now that you called, he thought to himself, grumbling more than usual. His nap, he could tell as he willed himself out of bed, had done nothing for his mental or physical condition.

"We're heading over to join them for dinner," Maroon's wife greeted him as he stumbled his way out of the bedroom and into the living room.

Maroon presumed she meant joining their daughter and grandson at their nearby residence. He didn't respond to her comment, though, instead just staring at his wife, not even able to assemble the thoughts to acknowledge or contradict her assertion.

Maroon's wife stared back at him, assessing her silent husband, before asking, "Are you up to it?"

Ninety-nine times out of a hundred, Maroon would have said *yes*. He loved times when his wife joined him, or he joined his wife, at their daughter's residence with their grandson at play. Usually, they took turns babysitting or otherwise visiting, to spread around both the opportunity and obligation, which they pursued and enjoyed daily. That's what made their time there together so special for Maroon, to have his whole family under one roof, just loving one another.

Yet on this day, Maroon wasn't even close to being up to it. He wasn't going. He couldn't.

"That's okay," his wife answered her own question in the face of Maroon's sullen silence. Seeing his distressed condition, she added consolingly, "We'll miss you. You go back to bed. You look like you need it. I'll bring you something."

Maroon listened for a note of irritation or condemnation in his wife's voice. But both were mercifully absent. Maroon therefore nodded glumly, turning slowly to slink back to the bedroom.

Maroon didn't want his wife to be concerned about him. He still expected to recover, he hoped without disclosure of the depths to which he had sunk, at least until after his recovery. Then, he'd speak of it with his wife. But he must look as bad as he felt, Maroon reasoned, or his wife would have shared her disappointment and urged Maroon to reconsider.

"Ná!" Maroon's grandson greeted Maroon's wife excitedly when she arrived at her daughter's house for dinner, minutes later. The little guy ran to embrace her at the door.

"Where's Pa?" Maroon's daughter asked her mother from the kitchen with a note of disappointment.

"Tired," Maroon's wife answered. Still hugging her grandson, she added, "He didn't look good. I told him to stay in bed."

Maroon's wife released her grandson from her hug. Sensing a tiresome adult conversation, he wandered back into the living room to resume his play, while keeping an ear on the conversation in case it involved him or other matters of consequence.

"He didn't look good when at the hollow, either," Maroon's daughter replied to her mother's disclosure, adding, "Are you worried about him?"

"Yes," Maroon's wife admitted.

"Can you get him to go to the doctor?" Maroon's daughter asked.

"Probably not, but I'll try," Maroon's wife replied.

"He was talking to himself again when we were at the hollow, or at least he was acting strangely," Maroon's daughter added.

Maroon's grandson, listening from the living room, silently shook his head but said nothing.

"I'm not worried about that," Maroon's wife replied, quickly changing the subject by adding, "He's in bed. He'll be better in the morning."

Back in bed at home, Maroon tossed and turned. His mind wanted him to get up and do something, even if only to sit in his office or on the back deck. His body and senses, though, told him he wasn't up to it and should stay in bed. And so he stayed in bed, trying to entertain his overactive mind with anything other than negative thoughts about his declining condition.

"Care for a visitor?" a deep voice addressed Maroon from the chair in the bedroom's corner.

Maroon looked over without surprise to see a stately gentleman seated in the chair. Maroon smiled. He was glad for a visitor, especially another visitor from beyond.

"I'm Robert Van Kampen," the gentleman said cordially.

Maroon instantly recognized the name, well known in present-day Grand Haven. A large, still-new-ish memorial stood in a newer part of the cemetery behind Maroon's residence, bearing the Van Kampen name. The good-sized burial plot the memorial marked had only one gravestone in it, that of Robert Van Kampen.

Maroon had never met Van Kampen, although he had been a visitor to a special part of Van Kampen's spectacular, lakeshore, dune-top Grand Haven residence.

Van Kampen had been an incredibly astute investment manager, earning himself and others many millions not only through skilled management but also with innovation. Van Kampen was the first to popularize packaging municipal bonds into insured trusts for individual investors.

Once Van Kampen had cracked the figurative code in the investment-management industry, he moved his office and residence from the Chicago area to Grand Haven. He could have lived and worked anywhere in the world. He chose Grand Haven, for his family's benefit.

Unfortunately, Van Kampen died of a viral infection of his heart at the young age of sixty, but not before blessing Grand Haven generously out of his considerable fortune and even greater commitments. The churches he founded, ones that his family members continued to lead and support, thrived. Van Kampen also supported local charities and public works with financial gifts few could afford, to both the immediate and long-lasting benefit of the community's citizens.

As much as Van Kampen did for the civic benefit of Grand Haven's residents, the private endeavor Van Kampen pursued with the greatest passion may well also have the most-lasting benefit. Van Kampen became a collector of impossibly rare Bible manuscripts and associated ancient documents. And he didn't just collect them as investments or for preservation. He also went to considerable cost and effort to make the documents available to scholars for biblical research and to the public for inspiration.

For a time, Van Kampen housed his rare manuscripts, the nation's best such collection, in an underground structure atop the lakeshore Grand Haven dunes on which he and his family lived, carefully constructed to preserve and display the manuscripts. Maroon had toured the facility as part of a small group of church leaders, marking the generosity with which Van Kampen made the materials available. Maroon was not in any sense a biblical scholar. He was instead just another fortunate beneficiary of Van Kampen's bottomless patronage.

As soon as Van Kampen introduced himself to Maroon in the dim light of his bedroom, the shutters of which Maroon had closed against the late afternoon's bright light, Maroon recalled his visit to Van Kampen's compound to see the collection. Among many other fascinating items, the collection included 4,000-year-old clay tablets and cuneiform, original translations from the 14th-Century hand of John Wycliffe, an old Bible stained with the blood of its former owner, and an authentic book of the Gutenberg Bible, the first major work printed on a press with moveable type. Curators had beautifully arranged the materials in the underground facility, to illustrate the incomparable text's story. The display had stunned Maroon, just as it had the visitors who accompanied him.

The Van Kampen family eventually moved the manuscripts to Florida.

Maroon smiled at Van Kampen, starting to sit up from bed out of respect for his esteemed visitor.

"No, no," Van Kampen discouraged Maroon, "You lay down. We'll just chat a bit if you don't mind, and then I'll get out of here so as not to disturb your rest. You just looked a little restless."

Maroon wanted to insist otherwise but felt himself incapable of objecting. He eased himself back down, facing Van Kampen, hoping the great man would speak freely without the necessity of Maroon's urging. Maroon had the sense that he was receiving a hospital visitation. If that was the context, then so be it, he reasoned. He wanted Van Kampen to stay and share.

"Thank you for letting us see your Bibles," Maroon managed to utter with considerable effort.

Van Kampen smiled, nodding in acknowledgment. He then proceeded to tell Maroon his inspiration for collecting the manuscripts, both out of his own passion for the original word and to aid and inspire others in its trustworthy study. Van Kampen wanted above all to know and embrace the truth, and he wanted to help others do so along with him. Although not trained as a scholar, he had researched and published several books on the vision and import of the incomparable text.

As Van Kampen spoke, Maroon's foggy mind just managed to follow the course of his account. Ordinarily, Maroon would have commented with his appreciation, while formulating question after question to guide their conversation along. But in his present troubled condition,

Maroon had only enough sense to track Van Kampen's words. No comments or questions came to mind. Maroon wouldn't have had the capability to utter them clearly if they had.

Van Kampen clearly knew of Maroon's disabled condition, which was obvious in any case. Much as a hospital visitor would avoid taxing the visited patient, Van Kampen moved from subject to subject, watching to see that Maroon was tracking him agreeably, entertained and eased of conscience rather than wearied and burdened. Such was the astute eye and good heart of the great financier.

Van Kampen shared with Maroon how his knowledge of scripture guided him in his business, financial, professional, family, and charitable matters. He shared how the scriptures had saved his life, made his marriage, helped him raise his children, and given him hope for the very future in the realm beyond that he now enjoyed. It was on that last subject that Van Kampen spent most of his time. Maroon soon understood, even in his badly weakened condition, that Van Kampen's primary subject, the end of life and the redemption of humankind and gorgeous but troubled creation in which humankind resided, was the point of Van Kampen's visit.

For a moment, Van Kampen's sharing aspects of his own demise and redemption alarmed Maroon. Maroon wondered whether Van Kampen's subject meant that Maroon was dying. Maroon had even heard an account of an angelic visitation to the hospital room of a dying acquaintance. Was Van Kampen Maroon's angel, bringing last words of assurance?

But Maroon managed to push the thought aside to focus on Van Kampen's impartation. Or it may have been that Maroon was too weak to hold two thoughts in mind at once, the first being his concern over his impending demise and the second being tracking Van Kampen's profound lesson. In any case, Maroon focused on the lesson, the teaching that Van Kampen seemed eager to impart.

Maroon was too weak to recall Van Kampen's words. He could not have related a reliable account of what Van Kampen actually said to him. But Maroon did later recall that Van Kampen's testimony had confirmed the ancient understanding, recorded in scripture, that Maroon had reached and accepted, of rescue from death followed by resurrection in one's transformed body. Maroon's Lord, who was also Van Kampen's Lord and the Lord of the transformed figures Maroon had hosted, was the way, truth, and life.

Maroon didn't need Van Kampen's testimony, in light of Van Kampen's own appearance and the appearances of the other figures from beyond, whose company Maroon had enjoyed over the prior days. But Van Kampen's account nonetheless helped Maroon connect the many dots between those visits and Maroon's scriptural understanding. For reasons he did not understand, Maroon had the privilege of seeing living proof of resurrection. He hadn't demanded it or perhaps even needed it. But he accepted it gladly and tried, with the little he had left in him, to show his appreciation to Van Kampen.

Just when Maroon was about to give out, Van Kampen rose, departing as quietly and gently as one would when ending a hospital visit that might be a final visit. Maroon later believed that Van Kampen had opened the bedroom door to quietly slip away, although he couldn't say for sure. Perhaps Van Kampen had walked through the door or even just slowly disappeared without movement. Van Kampen was no longer of this world but of the realm beyond. He could do as he thought best, without the material limitations of this world.

To his surprise, Maroon awoke the next morning, rather than later the same day of Van Kampen's visit. Maroon thought he remembered his wife checking on him when she returned from dinner at their daughter's house. But as with the disappearance of Van Kampen, Maroon could not be sure. Events and chronologies were becoming less and less clear.

The light sneaking through the bedroom's closed shutters suggested to Maroon that it was later in the morning than he usually rose. After cleaning up and dressing with great effort, he made his way to the kitchen, where he found his wife's note. She had taken the dogs for their morning walk. Some breakfast was on the counter. They could sit together when she returned, or they could go get some hot tea and a danish, whatever Maroon preferred. His wife signed the note with a heart.

Maroon knew instantly that the note was a significant indulgence, granted by his wife out of her concern over her husband's severe decline. Any other day, she simply would have rousted Maroon from bed with her characteristic *are you up?* even if Maroon rarely required such rousting. On this day, though, she had let him sleep in. Maroon couldn't recall it ever having happened. He must have looked as bad as he felt.

Maroon breathed a sigh of relief nonetheless, thinking that if this swift but cared-for decline was how his life was ending, then things would be alright. Not feeling up to eating the breakfast his wife had kindly prepared, as was her custom whether Maroon was ill or not, Maroon made his way to his office to sit for a bit, wait for his wife, and further clear his wits, if he was able. He had been in bed way longer than usual and had slept much longer than ever, without dreaming. He needed to sort himself out.

Maroon plopped himself down at his desk, fiddling with the mouse to wake up his computer so that he could start to write. Hadn't he left an assignment half finished? He couldn't recall. And if so, he didn't have the will or heart to take it up again.

"Let's just sit a while," a voice said from the couch across from Maroon's desk.

Maroon looked up from his computer to see his father-in-law, departed several years earlier, seated comfortably on the couch.

16

Maroon's wife had lost her dad some years earlier. Maroon and his wife had moved back to her Grand Haven hometown for several good reasons, including the town's safety, stability, civic spirit, good schools, and spectacular natural environment. His wife also had Grand Haven friends and history. But she also had her elderly and retired parents still living there.

Those parents meant at least two good things for Maroon and his wife. First, they could raise their daughter in her grandparents' care and company. To put it more pragmatically, Maroon and his wife had free and entirely trustworthy babysitting. But Maroon and his wife also wanted to care for her parents as they aged.

And care, the parents gradually required. Over the years, Maroon and his wife helped move them from their home to a condominium to an assisted living center to a nursing home. Another charm of Grand Haven is the high quality of its housing and residential care facilities for the elderly. Eventually, Maroon and his wife buried her parents. Grand Haven does that final service well, too, as Maroon knew from his church service and the passing of his own parents after having moved to Grand Haven for his family's care. The cemetery behind Maroon's residence stood as a timeless testament to the honor Grand Haven afforded its long-ago and recently departed residents.

Maroon's wife missed her parents. So did Maroon's daughter, who had graduated from college by the time of their passing, having spent many years in their care and caring for them along with Maroon and his wife. But Maroon's wife was especially close to her dad. She held his loss dear and held his memory closer. Without going into details, she had even received what she understood to be reassurances of his glorified ascension to the higher realm after his passing.

His wife's remembrance of her dad was Maroon's first thought on her dad's reappearance on the couch across from Maroon's desk. What would his wife think if she could see her father?

Maroon had a different relationship with his wife's dad, of course. His wife's dad had been a business leader, charitable leader, and pillar of the Grand Haven community, as previously mentioned. His wife's dad had no reason to believe Maroon to be his equal. Maroon had, after all, appeared out of nowhere to marry his daughter, at least nowhere close to Grand Haven. But his wife's dad nonetheless treated Maroon with kindness and respect at all times, even if he occasionally called Maroon by the wrong name, sometimes the name of a friend of his own and sometimes by the name of Maroon's wife's former boyfriend.

Maroon took in good spirits the tiny indignity his father-in-law occasionally imposed without any bad intention whatsoever. Maroon had every reason to look up, *way* up, to his wife's dad. And Maroon needed every good ground on which to maintain his own humility. Maroon was also forever indebted to his father-in-law, simply for raising such a fine daughter and having the grace or foolishness, whichever it was (and Maroon believed it be both), to allow Maroon to marry his daughter.

Maroon could thus not imagine that his wife's dad had returned simply to inform, inspire, or in some sense reassure Maroon. His wife's dad wouldn't have worried himself about Maroon at all, other than to ensure that Maroon did no harm to his daughter. Maroon immediately expected that his father-in-law's appearance instead had everything to do with Maroon's wife.

"You're looking well," Maroon found the words to address his father-in-law in the quiet, kind, easy, and confident manner Maroon had learned over the years to do so. He had always found it easy to chat with his father-in-law, even if not over serious things but in humorous or sympathetic small talk. Maroon gave him a warm smile.

His father-in-law returned the smile. Opening and closing his mouth a couple of times while preparing to talk, as was his natural manner, he soon replied, "How are you two doing?"

Maroon understood his father-in-law's question to mean *how my daughter is doing.* His father-in-law had simply couched his natural interest in his daughter's welfare in a more gracious package. Maroon, after all, was the one who was ill. Maroon, after all, was the one receiving these mysterious and, in the sense of his sharply declining health, progressively more ominous visitations, of which his father-in-law was now a part. The old man could have asked first after Maroon. But Maroon understood. It had always been that way between them, something Maroon appreciated as a greater degree of authenticity and candor, rather than construing it as deliberate disregard for Maroon's own value.

"She's fine, in fact doing very well," Maroon replied, answering the question his father-in-law had really intended to ask, while ignoring his own badly declined condition.

"Good to hear," the old man replied, adding, "I thought so."

After a moment's pause, and some more preparing to speak, while Maroon waited patiently, his father-in-law asked, "Say, could you do me a favor?"

"Sure," Maroon instantly answered, although internally, a small voice inside Maroon's head mockingly replied, *Of course I can while I'm dying here. Anything. Just ask anything, and I'll do it.* Maroon smiled at his internal voice, the devil on one shoulder, rejecting its sarcasm. He liked his father-in-law. He especially appreciated that his father-in-law wasn't going to beat around the bush, which Maroon was in no condition to tolerate.

"Could I see my daughter?" Maroon's father-in-law asked.

The question stunned Maroon, absolutely floored him. Making the question even more impactful, it appeared to Maroon that his father-in-law might have moist eyes, confirming what the question already revealed, that his father-in-law missed and longed for the company of his daughter.

Later, Maroon would realize that he had never considered how the figures who were visiting him from beyond might feel about the people their death had left behind or their offspring, future generations, or others in the earthly realm. But then, Maroon recognized how residents of the higher realm might long for their family members and others to join them. Of course, his wife's dad would miss her and want her to be with him again, except that he would never wish for that event when it meant leaving behind her other loved ones and her incomplete life on earth.

But in the moment, Maroon instantly answered, "Of course. She'll be home in a few minutes. Wait here with me, and she'll come in to see us. Or see me."

Maroon had to correct himself. He presumed that his wife would only see Maroon, not her dad, if the protocol of her dad's visit followed the protocol of the prior visits of Madame LaFramboise and the aviator Mars, two figures from beyond with whom his wife had unwittingly consorted in Maroon's witting presence.

Maroon's father-in-law nodded appreciatively. Maroon guessed that he had not spoken an answer, even to say *thank you*, because of the emotions he was trying to hide.

The next few minutes ensued in the kind of mundane conversation Maroon had usually shared with his father-in-law years ago. They didn't really discuss anything, at least not in any detail or depth. Their conversation was instead more like an exchange of familiar quips and witty replies, each bringing shared smiles to their faces. In this way, they gradually picked up in their relationship precisely where they had left off years earlier, with the older man's demise.

A couple of times during the brief course of their conversation, Maroon made comments or asked questions, an answer to which would have required his father-in-law to reveal conditions or events in heaven. Maroon noticed immediately that his father-in-law avoided responding to those comments or answering those questions in a way that would reveal anything of heaven. Apparently, the protocol for these rare, or as far as Maroon could tell *unprecedented*, earthly visits prohibited such disclosures.

Maroon would later consider, too, that these earthly visits of the departed actually seemed inconsistent with his understanding of the scriptures and their traditional interpretation and presentation. Yes, these appearances had convinced him of the reality of resurrection, although he had needed no convincing. But in point of fact, they had also introduced a wrinkle in his understanding, if not a contradiction of the scriptures, when Maroon knew better than to accept any such contradiction.

Maroon knew that knowledge on earth of such things is always incomplete. He trusted that events would, sooner or later, make these things clear, leaving no contradictions.

"Well, she should be home any minute," Maroon updated his father-in-law after a brief glance at his watch. Maroon added, "She's already overdue by her usual schedule."

"Oh!" the old man replied suddenly, "I almost forgot. I'm supposed to share something with you. Now, what was it?"

Maroon watched in amusement, and the tiniest bit of annoyance, as his father-in-law struggled to recall his message for Maroon.

"Did it have anything to do with my impending demise?" Maroon asked helpfully and with a pang of concern over the potential for an affirmative answer.

"No, no," his father-in-law replied, "That's not it."

"How about wisdom for living life?" Maroon asked, now beginning to tease his father-in-law in the way that he used to do, without his father-in-law necessarily knowing it.

"No, not exactly," the old man replied again, "Although now you're closer."

Maroon rattled off several platitudes, more to entertain himself with his ability to generate them and to tease his father-in-law than in any hope of triggering the necessary memory. After all, if Maroon knew what to suggest to his father-in-law, then he probably didn't need the message. He tried to trigger his father-in-law's recall nonetheless, beginning with *one day at a time* and continuing on with *live life to the fullest, give up to get back, don't sweat the small stuff, love those who love you, love your enemies as much as your friends*, and half a dozen other platitudes. None did the trick.

Maroon heard the garage door open for his wife's return, alerting his father-in-law, "Here she comes."

"Oh, shoot, then," the old man replied, "I'll let you know later if I think of your message."

Maroon nodded, chagrined but not offended. He was pretty sure by now that he didn't have a *later* to offer his father-in-law. Later would be too late. But the lesson he had already learned from his father-in-law long ago wasn't something he could put into words, anyway. It instead had something to do with his father-in-law's basic decency, not in all things at all times but in many things most of the time, when decency mattered more than anything else. A message from his father-in-law at this late date might have spoiled what his father-in-law had already taught Maroon, which is probably why Maroon's father-in-law had conveniently forgotten it.

"Honey, I'm home!" Maroon heard his wife call from the garage door, "Are you up?"

Maroon smiled, thinking *if I wasn't up when you called, I would be now*. He began to rise with difficulty from his office chair to go greet her but then remembered that he wanted her to come back to the office where her dad awaited.

"Can you come back here when you get a minute?" Maroon hollered back to his wife, while still seated at his desk in the office, across from which sat his wife's dad.

"Everything alright?" she shouted back.

"Fine!" Maroon hollered back again with effort, adding, "Just come back here when you get a minute!"

Maroon listened from his office desk, hearing his wife get fresh water for the dogs, change her shoes, head to the other end of the house for something, and return to the kitchen for a drink. Her dad fidgeted on the couch, clearly excited for his daughter's appearance in the office doorway.

When Maroon heard the vacuum begin to run, he made the great effort of rising, while saying with a sheepish look toward his father-in-law, "I'll go get her."

The old man nodded understandingly. Maroon guessed that things had pretty much worked the same way in his own house. Like mother, like daughter.

A moment later, Maroon reappeared in the office door, his wife in tow and explaining, "I was just cleaning up stuff that the dogs tracked in."

"That's alright, Honey," Maroon replied sweetly, "I just needed to see you for a minute."

Maroon slipped into the office ahead of his wife to settle with great relief back down at his desk. His wife stood in the office door, expectantly, presumably waiting for Maroon to announce his needs. Without making it obvious, Maroon watched his father-in-law's expression out of the corner of his eye, while trying to think of how to gently coax his wife into the office without irritating her and spoiling the moment for her dad. Her dad was staring at his daughter, mouth open, eyes watering. Seeing his expression, Maroon had to hold back his own tears.

"Can you come in for just a minute and sit on the couch?" Maroon said gently to his wife.

"Are you alright?" she replied, still standing in the doorway.

Maroon nodded but made a gentle motion with his hand, inviting his wife to enter and sit.

"I could come back for as long as you want if you can just give me a few more minutes to pick things up," Maroon's wife insisted.

Maroon stole another glance at his father-in-law out of the corner of his eye, this time seeing that he was weeping. Maroon looked quickly away so as not to join him in tears.

"Just stay for a minute," Maroon repeated, making the same inviting motion with his hand.

Maroon's wife finally relented. Without more protest than a small pursing of her lips, and to Maroon's great relief, she finally entered the office, made her way around the desk to the couch, and took a seat on it at the opposite end from her dad, who sat staring and weeping.

Maroon smiled at his wife, trying again not to join her dad in tears.

"I just wanted to say I love you," Maroon told his wife honestly, unable to think of anything else to say. Their conversation wasn't the point, although his wife was unaware of it.

"Are you sure you're alright?" she replied, adding, "You sound so serious. And you slept for how long yesterday and last night? Are you feeling any better? You look a little better. Why don't you just tell me what you want?"

Maroon was glad for his wife's chatter. He didn't think he could have held it together if he had to speak again. Her dad's sobs, though, had slowed. But the old man still stared at his daughter, now shaking his head in wonder.

Maroon summoned his strength and senses to speak again. But now he knew he couldn't do so. He instead reached a hand across the desk, holding it open for his wife's hand. She took it hesitantly. He squeezed it lightly and let it go.

"That's it?" she asked gently.

Maroon nodded. He had a thousand other things to tell her, a thousand last words to share, a thousand last memories to recall, but he spoke none of them, knowing that he couldn't do so, and knowing that their conversation wasn't the point of her visit to the office that Maroon had compelled.

"Are you sure that's it?" she asked, adding, "I mean, we could go see the doctor, or we could take a walk or take a drive. I don't have to clean the house right now. It can wait."

Maroon wanted to do all the things his wife had just suggested. Maroon wanted to pour himself out to his wife in love and concern, guidance and caution, and exhortation and memory. But Maroon didn't think he was up to any of it or that any of it would change his circumstance or hers. Maroon thought instead of his father-in-law's basic decency.

What would the old man sitting across the desk from him on the couch beside his daughter have done under these same circumstances of his impending demise? Maroon knew that he would have told his wife that he loved her. He would have squeezed her hand lightly. And he would have encouraged her to return to her happy routines while he prepared himself for his final departure.

Maroon's wife rose to leave. As she walked past Maroon's desk, she paused to lean over and kiss him on the top of his head. She then stepped to the office doorway.

"Hey, one last thing," Maroon said quietly to her, with all the sense and clarity he could muster.

His wife stopped in the doorway and turned back to him, leaving her perfectly framed in the doorway for her dad to regard in full wonder. Maroon gathered himself to speak, hoping that he could hold it together long enough to hear her response, and hoping even more that her response was what he thought it would be.

17

"Do you think of your dad often?" Maroon asked his wife, as she stood framed in his office doorway.

Maroon had to bite his lip to keep from weeping as he waited for her answer. Fortunately, though, as soon as Maroon had mentioned her father, she had looked up and out of the office windows, across the gorgeous rolling dune over which Madame LaFramboise had walked so long ago and so recently.

Maroon watched his wife stand silently in the office doorway, gazing out across the cemetery. Her dad likewise sat mesmerized on the couch, staring lovingly at his daughter. Finally, after what seemed like an eternity, she blinked several times, Maroon guessed to hold back tears, and answered.

"I speak to him all the time," Maroon's wife replied, "He's with me always."

And with her answer, all three of them were sobbing. Immediately, Maroon's wife turned to leave. Maroon let her go, lowering his own head into his hands. When he looked up, his father-in-law was gone. He was once again alone in his office.

Maroon remained seated in his office, letting the flood of emotions slowly recede without in any way hurrying them off.

Soon, though, Maroon thought more clearly of the implications of his wife's answer. His wife had been relatively quick to excuse and even to defend his talking to himself, as she understood it, when he had been talking to his otherworldly visitors over the several prior days. She hadn't troubled him over it. And Maroon now realized why not. Because she spoke to and lived in the continuous presence of her dad. She had her own closest companion from the realm beyond, with her daily, one whom only she, not Maroon, could see and hear.

Maroon's wife carried her father within her, reflecting his basic decency and other transmitted commitments. She conversed with him daily, informing her attitudes and actions, while building her own legacy to transmit.

Yet Maroon's father-in-law, his wife's dad, also lived within Maroon, even if Maroon didn't see and talk with him daily. Maroon's father-in-law, for instance, helped Maroon to act decently when his passions urged him to do otherwise. Maroon's father-in-law also helped Maroon to temper his overbearing penchant for control through explanation. Presence was often enough, even far better, than messages and explanations.

The historical figures who visited Maroon, though, had taught him not just what it means to live within a family but to live within a place. Maroon had learned what it means to draw on the legacy of the historic figures who influence and establish the character of a place, through the culture its residents share and transmit. Never mind culture, though, as a means of transmission. Culture is a figment of imagination. The people who establish and foster a community are the ones who transmit.

The town founder Reverend Ferry thus also lived within and beside Maroon, his wife, and their daughter. Reverend Ferry had transmitted a reverence for the beauty of Grand Haven, within Maroon, his wife, and their daughter. Reverend Ferry would soon also live within Maroon's grandson, as the little guy matured as a Grand Haven resident. Reverend Ferry had loved and sacrificed for Grand Haven with a peculiar set of commitments that the community embraced and continues to celebrate, at times consciously but always subconsciously.

Rix Robinson also lived within Maroon, his wife, and their daughter, whether they recognized it so readily as the better-known founder Ferry or not. Robinson's desire not only to draw richly from Grand Haven, whether in game, fish, furs, or trade, but also to let Grand Haven draw richly from Robinson, was in the DNA of Maroon, his wife, and their daughter. Maroon and his family received untold riches of beauty, provision, security, stability, faith, care, and love from Grand Haven, while more than willing to let

Grand Haven draw from them what it most needed or desired.

Robinson had even drawn River Woman from Grand Haven, as a sacred and lifelong gift, while he gave himself to River Woman in equal sacrifice. But River Woman also lived within Maroon, his wife, and their daughter. River Woman taught the Grand Haven community to treat its spectacular natural environment as sacred creation. She also taught the community to turn the benefits of that sacred creation back to the highest being, the author of creation. Maroon and his family walked through the town's woods and over its dunes knowing that they walked in the riches of their creator.

Maroon also carried within him the character and commitments of Robert Duncan, Grand Haven's first lawyer. Duncan's wife Martha had only recently shared with Maroon her husband's rare insight to let one's purpose draw meaning from the future. But having lived and practiced law in Duncan's Grand Haven while walking in Duncan Woods so often, Maroon had already acquired and pursued Duncan's insight. Maroon found himself constantly training the passion of his purpose on the landscape of the future, to find the meaning Maroon needed to thrive.

As he sat in his office, expending his last small energies reflecting on each of the historical figures who had visited him, Maroon next came upon the teacher Mary White, whose Grand Haven community had been whispering her wisdom to Maroon since he first set foot within the town's borders. Miss White had lived her life as she urged Maroon to do, participating through her resolute, faith-driven, and highly skilled teaching, in the broadest and deepest form of the divine liturgy. Maroon could sense that liturgy not merely while in glorious worship in church but also as it hung gorgeously in the air of Grand Haven.

The lumberman Dwight Cutler had inherited and extended Miss White's insight. He wrought a celebrated Grand Haven life that proved the power of full and fitting participation in that divine liturgy. Cutler had received, done, and given back more than a dozen good men, perhaps a hundred of them, by devoting his full attention to the quotidian details of effective Grand Haven commerce. Maroon had inherited that personal industry when pursuing his own craft in Grand Haven's business and professional community, although Maroon had only recently learned the broad outline of the remarkable life of Dwight Cutler.

In his seafaring across the Great Lakes, Captain Loutit had modeled for Maroon, his family, and every other member of the Grand Haven community his own advice to participate within the structure of being. Loutit had turned his natural restlessness from frivolous wandering into fruitful transport. He had carried with him across the waters not his own foolishness but goods and provisions to build new communities and sustain old ones. Maroon, his wife, and their daughter had inherited Loutit's gift, turning their own restless itches into carrying the concerns and burdens of others off across the healing waters. They had unknowingly followed the pattern and pathway of the fruitful seafarer who had blessed their community with both his fortunes and model.

The first cottage builder Mrs. Saunders had also woven her pattern into the fabric of Grand Haven's community, to warm and inform Maroon and his family. Mrs. Saunders'

Highland Park community and cottage stood high above Maroon's residence, hidden in the dune forest, as a witness to the opportunities one can seize when looking past the demands of the moment. Her quaint cottage along the route to the beach silently reminded Maroon, his family, and the rest of their lakeshore community that the lakeshore is a place of security, peace, and rest, not just a place of great commercial opportunity. Maroon and his family had drawn from the Highland Park spirit of the place that Mrs. Saunders had modeled so well.

For his part, Healy Akeley had shown Grand Haven how to look as far forward as one can, projecting the commercial profit of today far into the future through the charitable training of the next generation of young women. He saw that the love, care, service, character, and acumen of those young women would determine the integrity of the families on whom Grand Haven depended for its future. By pouring his fortunes into those young women, he was ensuring not just their health and welfare but the future of every child they would bear and raise in Grand Haven, and their grandchildren. Akeley had seeded the soil in which the mother of Maroon's wife could raise a daughter of such great character, who with Maroon would raise another daughter of the same character, who would raise her son, Maroon's grandson, with the same character.

The seaman O'Malley had flavored the intoxicating Grand Haven brew with a salty character. O'Malley had shown how a seaman's courage to draw life from deadly chaos waters can be the nourishing wine that both opens and closes the community's communion circle. O'Malley had modeled the right grip. He had shown how to hold on for dear life to the essentials, while letting go of the things that should rightly sink deep below the waters. Maroon and his family had acquired O'Malley's courage, care for his community, and remembrance of fallen comrades.

Madame LaFramboise had shown Grand Haven how to bring its disparate parts together into a healthy whole. The bounty she drew from her remarkable cross-cultural adaptations proved to the community how its members could live peacefully and purposely together, despite having different ancestors who spoke different languages following different customs. Madame LaFramboise had shown how to integrate the best aspects of one's several worlds into a whole and healthy life. Maroon and his family had inherited her openness to difference as a path to unified and whole life, just as had the Grand Haven community, which welcomed Dutch immigrants, Spanish-speaking migrants, and others, to undertake fruitfully their own efforts to preserve and integrate the best of their available worlds.

The aviator Mars had also woven his wild spirit into Grand Haven's fabric, showing how taking flight from home can be to show home the greater possibilities the sky offers. He had pointed the Grand Haven community up and outward, showing its members that the horizon is our destiny, not that we must leave home but that we must point our home and take our home to the realm beyond. Mars had shown how to find a home in the sky, letting the realm beyond feed the home inside. Maroon and his family had drawn from Mars' fanciful flights, turning their own fanciful flights toward home.

The athlete Ball had blessed Grand Haven with its sense of play. Ball had reminded the community not just to build bars, shops, offices, and factories but also diamond ball fields nestled into the base of dunes. Ball's spirit is at every Grand Haven youth sports game and practice, at every ice arena, basketball court, and football or soccer field. Maroon and his family had drawn frequently from Ball's playful spirit, to balance their lives and revitalize their energies.

The great jurist Epaphroditus Ransom had in his own indomitable way stood tall over Grand Haven for generations, reminding its citizens that the community's measure is in how it treats the weakest and least. Ransom had given his life for justice, for the slave's liberty, leaving a legacy that calls us each to stand for what we know, as the one way to free us from our oppressions. Maroon and his family had drawn from Ransom's witness, discerning oppressions to stand against, drawing on what they knew was freely available for all.

Van Kampen had also shaped the character of the Grand Haven community, not just with his generosity but also with his passion for the word of life and reason, the breath and spirit of the Lord. Van Kampen had directed his passion and purpose toward the realm beyond, where his passion and purpose would have the greatest impact on the greatest number for the longest time, which happens to be eternity. Maroon, his family, and the Grand Haven community had drawn most deeply on Van Kampen's legacy, devoted to the word of life.

Slumped in his chair at his desk, Maroon had no further thoughts. He had welcomed each visitor from beyond as best as he could manage. He had listened carefully, ensuring that he understood and would remember their messages. But more than simply noting their words, he had embraced their spirit, letting their character and personality draw firmer and straighter his own soul.

Maroon understood that we live and learn not just by lessons but also through the people who impart them. He now saw that these figures had been living inside him all along, ever since he had moved to Grand Haven and begun to draw on its history, culture, character, and civic commitments. Maroon had benefited enormously from them, without hardly knowing them and without having credited them. How much better might he have lived, how much more might he have done for his family, and how much better might he have served and cared for others, if he had pursued them and learned from them earlier? And what other figures had he missed?

But it no longer mattered. Maroon closed his eyes at peace and at rest.

"Hey, Pa!" his daughter's voice called from the garage door, "We're here for a visit!"

Maroon stirred but without the energy to rise. He could no longer force himself from his seat and so didn't try. Indeed, he lacked the energy even to call back to his daughter, hoping instead that she would make her way back to his office.

Maroon heard his daughter coaxing her son into entering the home, saying, "Let's go see Papa."

A moment later, the two of them were at the office door. The little guy pushed his way past his mom to slip around the desk and flop on the couch, saying, "Can we watch cartoons, Papa?"

Maroon smiled as his only response, wanting to say *yes* but lacking the energy.

"No," his mother answered her son's question, even though he had directed it to Maroon. She added quietly, "We're not watching cartoons. Let's just say hi to Papa for a minute."

The little guy didn't fuss back at his mom, as he ordinarily might have. He instead watched his mom enter the office to move gently to Maroon, still slumped in his seat but wearing a wan smile of appreciation for their presence. Maroon's daughter leaned over to kiss Maroon's head, just as Maroon's wife had done when she had risen from the couch to depart the office earlier that morning.

"Come on, Son," Maroon's daughter said to her little guy, "Papa's tired. Give him a hug, and let's go."

Maroon's grandson slid off the couch, walked around the desk, and gave Maroon a hug. Maroon wanted to lift his grandson onto his lap for a proper hug and to wrestle with him but didn't have the energy even to lift his arms to return the little guy's hug. He just smiled weakly at him, while blinking back tears.

"Come on, Son," Maroon's daughter cajoled the little guy, who turned and walked from the office.

Maroon's daughter smiled at Maroon one last time, patted him gently on the shoulder, and turned to follow her son out of the office.

Maroon took a deep breath, closing his eyes. He heard the door to the garage open and his daughter coaxing her son out the door. But a moment later, the little guy reappeared at the office door.

"Papa," he called to Maroon, staring at Maroon slumped in his seat at the desk. When Maroon didn't move or open his eyes, the little guy repeated, "Papa."

Maroon thought he heard a call. He opened his eyes to see his grandson standing beside his office chair. Maroon smiled at him. The little guy was saying something, though. Maroon struggled to make it out.

"Papa," the little guy repeated, "Will you come see me like the others when you're gone?"

The little guy's voice made its way deep inside Maroon, who finally grasped what he was saying. With great effort, Maroon replied, "Oh yes, I will. I will. Just call me, and I'll be there."

Maroon tried to lift a hand to the little guy's shoulder but couldn't.

"It's alright, Papa," Maroon's grandson said.

Maroon's daughter called from the door to the garage. The little guy turned and ran from the room. Maroon watched him go and then closed his eyes to the sound of the door to the garage closing. He was alone. He was done.

18

Maroon remained slumped at his desk, knowing he could no longer speak or move. When he managed to open his eyes, the computer screen stared blankly back at him, waiting for him to lift his hands to the keyboard to pour forth more life. But Maroon couldn't do so. Maroon could no longer speak or write. He could no longer breathe his words into the world, carrying the spirit he had within him. Indeed, he could no longer hear or read the words of others, breathing in their spirits to live within him.

When Maroon had been a lawyer, his writing had direct impacts on the lives of the people whom he served. His writing formed contracts and corporations through which his clients managed their business affairs. He also wrote court complaints, motions, and briefs, and even opening statements, closing arguments, and jury instructions, that advocated his clients' causes for justice. His legal writing influenced outcomes, fostered relationships, repaired rifts, and restored order. Writing as a lawyer involved Maroon deeply in the world.

When Maroon had been a law professor, his writing had no longer served the immediate interests of clients. Instead, his writing had communicated to students the collective wisdom of the ages, so that those students could take their new knowledge, skills, and judgment to serve the interests of their clients. Maroon had written outlines, worksheets, articles, textbooks, and exams, things that would help no client but would help new lawyers help clients. Maroon was a step removed from the world but, through writing, still involved in it.

As his capacities waned nearer the end of his life, Maroon no longer had the vitality for physical labor nor even for getting to the school or office. Yet Maroon continued to write, alone in his office. He wrote educational content for law firms to share over the internet. He also wrote his own books and web materials, trying to encourage others from afar. Maroon was two steps removed from the world but still writing to play any small part in it.

When no one seemed any longer to need or want Maroon's involvement in the world, Maroon continued to write. Writing remained his life. Writing became his way of assuring himself that he was living. Writing also became his way of processing and remembering the words of others. Maroon was three steps removed from the world.

He had no role in the world but was still cognizant of it through writing.

Now, though, Maroon could no longer write to share with others nor write to accept what others had shared. He was done. His end was at hand. The computer screen was dark. Indeed, Maroon realized as he opened his eyes again, the screen had entirely disappeared. So had the keyboard and mouse. And where was his desk and the couch across from it?

Maroon stirred to rise but realized that his chair had disappeared, too. He looked around the office only to discover that his office was gone. Its walls had disappeared. Maroon looked helplessly for anything solid, anything familiar. He had sight but saw nothing.

Except that Maroon could see something. He could see a crowd of figures around him. Yes, there were Healy Akeley and James Mars. And there, Epaphroditus Ransom. And there, Neal Ball and Madame LaFramboise. Reverend Ferry and Rix Robinson, River Woman, and Mary White were there, too, along with Dwight Cutler, Martha Duncan, and Robert Van Kampen. Mars, O'Malley, Loutit, and Mrs. Saunders were there, too, all circled around him.

"What do you think, Maroon?" O'Malley laughed, "Want to join us?"

"Cat's got his tongue," Ball answered, adding with a great guffaw at his own humor, "First time ever for a lawyer."

"Oh, hey, Maroon," Cutler teased jovially, "Did you ever finish that last wood project? We picked out some good stock for you."

"No," Akeley answered in jest for Maroon, with a good laugh of his own, "He was too busy writing."

"Leave him alone, guys," Mary White admonished in mock seriousness, "Or I'll box your ears so good you won't hear for a week."

"Yes," Martha Duncan chimed in gently, "Leave poor Maroon alone until he's come to his senses. You know these things take some adjustment."

On the banter went around Maroon, much of it about him, much of it recounting joys, laughs, adventures, and hearty interactions the figures had shared with one another and others in the mysterious realm Maroon had now fully joined. Maroon watched and listened, astounded and enthralled, but feeling oddly bodiless, as if having no voice with which to speak and no appendages with which to move.

Gradually, though, Maroon started to breathe. He was indeed present among the welcoming figures. And gradually, Maroon started to move. He had a body after all.

Maroon jumped when a hand touched him on his shoulder, a shoulder he was only gradually realizing he had for someone to touch. Maroon turned to see Madame LaFramboise, who let her hand linger on Maroon's shoulder. She looked across Maroon to a figure on his other side.

"I think he's coming around, Epaphroditus," Madame LaFramboise said across Maroon to Ransom standing on the other side of him.

In response, Ransom took Maroon's hand to give it a good shake, holding on after the handshake was done.

Maroon felt Ransom's grasp in a hand he was only then realizing he had. Maroon tried squeezing his hand around Ransom's continued grasp.

Ransom smiled, saying to Madame LaFramboise, "Oh, yes. Now he's got it. He is indeed coming around."

"Catch!" Ball suddenly called to Maroon from a short distance away, just as he tossed a baseball in Maroon's direction.

Maroon flinched but utterly failed to move his free hand in time to catch or divert the ball. The ball thumped Maroon in the abdomen, fell at his feet, and rolled slowly away.

"Now stop that," Mary White scolded Ball with mock severity, although she wore a knowing smile.

"See, look," Ball replied to Miss White, pointing at Maroon and adding with a big grin, "He tried to catch it. I'll have him swinging a bat in no time, maybe cross-handed."

"No cross-handed swings for this gentleman," Reverend Ferry said grandly. He stepped to Maroon's side where Madame LaFramboise had just glided away, to place his arm over Maroon's shoulder. Ferry added with a confident smile at Maroon, "He's a straight shooter, this one, not like some of these knuckleheads."

Maroon felt the reassuring weight of the reverend's arm across his shoulders. He could see what his new celestial friends were doing, acclimating him to their realm, helping him recognize his form and reassume his personality.

"Hey, who are you calling a knucklehead?" Robinson replied to Ferry in mock indignation, although he wore a great smile.

"No one in particular," Ferry instantly replied, adding with a chuckle, "Although my comment seems to have found a suitable taker."

The reverend's wit drew guffaws from Ball and appreciative laughter not only from Akeley, Cutler, O'Malley, and Mars but also Robinson.

"Friends, friends," a kind but commanding voice called from behind Maroon.

The jocularity of the figures instantly stopped, not in fear but in hushed reverence, as they all turned toward the call. All lowered their heads. Ransom bowed deeply, while Mrs. Saunders curtsied. Cutler and Akeley slowly kneeled together. Ball and O'Malley lay prostrate. Maroon heard a gorgeous quiet song arise, coming from Mary White, joined by Martha Duncan, both of whom kneeled, faces down.

Reverend Ferry removed his arm from across Maroon's shoulders and stepped back, allowing Maroon to turn, too, to see who had spoken. Ferry then kneeled, face to the ground.

As Maroon turned, he expected to see a glorious king, priest, or commander. Maroon instead made out an ordinary-looking man of the simplest attire, seeming at once both perfect in form and proportion, so obviously untainted and sterling as to be without blemish, but also somehow utterly broken, and thus both the image and end of human form, while also divine.

Maroon knew the one on whom he looked. Maroon, like the other figures around him, felt his head pleased to bow, his knees glad to give way, and his face delighted to touch the ground in the figure's utter reverence and complete honor.

The perfectly broken man began to speak, calmly, cordially, in a voice so familiar to Maroon that he felt as if the man was his own father, his own brother, his own child, and his own soul.

As the perfect man spoke, Maroon felt himself naturally rising again to his feet, not because he had completed an obligatory act of honor but because to remain prostrate would have been to dishonor the perfect man's speech. Maroon could see that the others had risen, too, although Maroon and the others all retained reverential postures.

"Welcome, my friend, to the true realm," the perfect man began, addressing Maroon. He added, "I can see that your other friends here have already helped you acquaint yourself with your transcendent local form."

Maroon nodded, more in the manner of a small and solemn bow. The perfect man's words didn't so much fall on Maroon's ears but pierce gently and swiftly straight to his soul, demanding a delicious consent. But the perfect man was continuing.

"You should understand, now that you are fully here, that you were already experiencing the true realm when these friends were sharing their individual visits with you over these past several days," the perfect man explained. He continued, "I do not send my resurrected images to the realm below. I instead send my divine entities to carry out my earthly wishes. But I do sometimes draw my friends from the realm below to this true realm through the gentle individual introductions of my resurrected images, as was the case with you."

The perfect man paused in his address to Maroon, giving Maroon a moment to digest what he had just heard and to adjust his former thinking.

Indeed, Maroon had received his many recent celestial visits as if he still lived on earth, when what he had just now learned was that he had already withdrawn from earth into the realm above when receiving those visitors. For a moment, Maroon wondered how his earthly life seemed to have continued, even in the company and endearment of his wife, daughter, and grandson. But the perfect man was already answering, or explaining why he would not yet fully answer, the question Maroon had just formulated.

"You will gradually discover many new things about this true realm and about the nature of the realm below," the perfect man resumed, adding, "But you should also know that many things here and below will remain unknown."

Maroon once again nodded deeply in solemn acknowledgement. Maroon silently mused that he just might soon learn more about how his passing had occurred within such wonders. But once again, clearly having anticipated or more likely outright read Maroon's thoughts, the perfect man was already explaining.

"Receive the things I disclose without troubling yourself about the things I withhold," the perfect man continued, "For my revelation occurs always and only when you are ready to receive it, a revelation that will continue on forever in this true realm."

Maroon let the perfect man's words once again pierce him like the sharpest of double-edged swords, sundering his joints and marrow, dividing even his soul and spirit, not painfully but as a skilled surgeon would repair the slightest disordering of those members.

Once again, the perfect man spoke, this time, though, with words that seemed only to flow into Maroon, not out into the realm, to the ears or knowledge of the others still gathered around him.

"When your earthly family bestowed your name, you received it only with earthly knowledge," the impartation began, continuing with, "When I began to draw you to this true realm through these friends, you learned a little of your name's true meaning. I now reveal your name in this realm and its full meaning."

Maroon took a deep breath in anticipation, like a fielder ready to run after a long fly ball or a batter ready to swing at an incoming fastball. But the perfect man's revelation wasn't a target that Maroon had to follow in vain effort to grasp or hit. Instead, the perfect man's revelation of Maroon's own name and the profound meaning of that name flowed directly into Maroon's soul, taking its residence there as the disclosure of Maroon's already formed person.

Maroon wouldn't have been able to relate the revelation he received. Words, as they say, would never do it justice. Yet if, as a resolute and skilled writer, he had made the attempt, then it would have included the things he had learned about himself from his recent celestial encounters, having to do with the color of spilled blood, and of resoluteness and passion. But Maroon's inexact and insufficient description of his name's revelation would also have included other things, having to do with very grand havens.

Deep in the revelation of his authentic name, Maroon also perceived more of the world's fractal structure, each little part representing the whole and thus not being little at all, while the whole represented each little part and was thus not so grand as to be incomprehensibly remote and distant. Maroon saw deep within the revelation that his miniscule story of earthly birth, heavenly rebirth, and earthly sacrifice adequately, if clearly imperfectly, reflected the perfect man's cosmological grand narrative, indeed the perfect man's own story as creation's author.

Maroon saw that he mattered, his life mattered, because his story was the grand story, although in infinitesimal and distorted but nonetheless suitable reflection. Maroon also saw that the perfect man was both the author and subject of the cosmological story, not alone, but in union with his Father and their breath between them, and not solely for their own purpose but also for the perfect love of their human images including Maroon.

Both stricken by and made whole from the divine transmission, Maroon prepared to bow again in solemn acknowledgement of the perfect man's generous revelations, so generous as to have been made at the expense of the perfect man's own blameless life. But the perfect man had already turned to address the other figures.

"Should I give our new friend a glimpse of the coming redemption of his former residence?" he asked the other figures, adding with a beatific smile, "His Grand Haven was your former residence, too."

Exhilarated cheers erupted from the figures. Ball jumped up and down in exaggerated excitement. Reverend Ferry and Martha Duncan held their arms aloft in sheer exultation. Mrs. Saunders held her hands over her mouth, stifling shouts of joyful anticipation. O'Malley danced a jig, pulling a laughing Cutler and Loutit around in circles with him. Madame LaFramboise held her arms wide, ready to embrace the vision of her beloved Grand Haven home in its fully redeemed splendor.

Maroon stared in wonder at the wild excitement of his new friends from this realm beyond. He hardly understood what the perfect man had offered. A glimpse of Grand Haven's *coming redemption*? Wasn't Grand Haven already special enough? What could be its *redemption*? Maroon even less understood the eruption of joy around him. What marvel could so excite, like little children, these noble, regal, already redeemed and transformed celestial residents?

But then Maroon remembered the word's final revelation. He remembered the fruit-bearing trees, streets of gold, and foundations of precious stones. He remembered the divine entities of fearsome form and the legions in glorious worship. And he remembered the descent of the celestial city. Yes, Grand Haven, too, would receive its redemption, every branch and twig, every blade of grass, every rolling dune.

Maroon watched as the perfect man raised his arms, revealing for only an instant what earth can neither see nor speak, for the shattering wonder of its glory.

19

Maroon's wife and daughter walked back together from the graveside service interring Maroon's body in his beloved cemetery. The gravesite wasn't anywhere near the gravesites of the celestial figures Maroon had welcomed, described in the above account. Those graves were in the cemetery's older and more-venerable locations. But Maroon's remains now lay buried in the same rolling dunes over which he and his wife had so often walked behind their residence, overlooking the grand cemetery.

Maroon's daughter had left her little guy with a friend, sparing him the sight of the casket's ceremonial lowering into the ground. She had been uncertain of his capacity to process that aspect of his Papa's passing, although the little guy had attended the church memorial service, which seemed more suited to his young mind and special needs.

On her stroll back to Maroon's former residence with her mother, Maroon's daughter realized, though, that her little guy would have rather enjoyed the outdoor scenery, the hike, the cemetery's mechanical equipment, and the great sand pit the backhoe had dug, over the boredom and physical constraint of the indoor church memorial service. The little guy probably would have run off after birds, dogs, and insects during the graveside service, but his mom would have let him do so, believing that it would be his own way of honoring his Papa with whom he had hiked so often through these same dunes.

Maroon's wife and daughter had little to say to one another on their stroll back to the residence. Of course, the few days since Maroon's passing had exhausted them with memorial preparations and other administrative duties. The challenge of bearing a death can initially be more in its administration than in the loss, which may not sink in until days or even weeks later.

When they arrived back at the residence, Maroon's daughter entered with her mother, wanting to be sure that her mother was alright before leaving to pick up her little guy from the friend who was caring for him. Maroon's wife urged her daughter on her way after the little guy, whose presence would have reassured both of them.

As Maroon's daughter prepared to leave, she peeked into Maroon's old office. The chair in which Maroon had spent so many hours, indeed so many years, sat empty, staring at the darkened computer screen, with the keyboard and mouse abandoned on the desk between them.

Maroon's daughter sat in her dad's chair, looking not at the black computer screen but instead out the windows to the cemetery's rolling green expanse. How curious, she thought, that anyone would want to look out their residence's windows on a cemetery. But how perfect and poignant that view had become for Maroon, his wife, and his daughter, his daughter also thought.

Maroon's daughter leaned forward in her dad's old chair, placing her chin in her hands with her elbows propped on the desk, to continue to gaze out the windows at the cemetery, across which she could just make out the Civil War soldier statute and, beyond it, the overlook on which the town had buried its founder and first teacher.

But as she did so, her elbow bumped the mouse. And with the mouse's movement, the computer screen popped on from its timed slumber. On the screen was a manuscript, bearing the filename *Grand Haven*. She began scrolling through the manuscript, soon seeing that it told extraordinary tales of encounters with the town's historical figures.

"I thought you left," Maroon's wife said to her daughter, as she appeared in the office doorway. When her daughter simply looked up from the computer without rising, Maroon's wife added, "You'd better be getting on your way."

"You should probably see this," her daughter replied, motioning toward the computer screen.

Maroon's wife leaned over to get a view of the screen. Shrugging, she said, "Another book?"

Maroon's daughter nodded. Knowing that her mother didn't read Maroon's writings and might not read this one even if she suggested it, Maroon's daughter simply asked, "May I send this file to myself to read more of it later?"

Maroon's wife shrugged again, replying as she turned and left, "Sure. Tell me if you find anything important."

Maroon's daughter made a few swift keystrokes, sending access to the file to her own email. She then popped up to head out after her son, leaving the computer on, knowing that it would soon return to sleep and later get unplugged and discarded.

"We'll swing by to check on you later," Maroon's daughter called to her mother as she left.

"That's alright, Honey," she heard the reply, "You get some rest and I'll see you two tomorrow."

Maroon's daughter and her son returned the next day to check on Maroon's wife, although of course, Maroon's daughter had sent her mother several reassuring texts through the evening and early the next morning.

"How are you holding up?" Maroon's daughter asked her mother quietly when they arrived, while her son fussed with the dogs.

"Fine, I think," Maroon's wife replied absentmindedly, instead giving her attention to her grandson.

Maroon's daughter let the two of them play with the dogs for a while. Maroon's wife soon propped her grandson up in the big bed in the master bedroom watching cartoons, while she returned to the kitchen to make him lunch.

"I read the story last night, the one he left open on the computer," Maroon's daughter related as her mother moved about the kitchen.

"Oh?" Maroon's wife replied disinterestedly, adding, "What did you find?"

"He wrote of meeting Reverend Ferry, Mary White, and other long-gone figures here at home or around the cemetery," her daughter replied.

"Really?" Maroon's wife asked without interrupting her lunch preparations. She hesitated a moment, though, asking, "Are you hungry? Do you want me to make you some?"

Maroon's daughter shook her head, replying instead, "He also wrote about asking you if you thought of your Papa a lot."

Maroon's wife stopped, her daughter finally having caught her attention. Maroon's daughter resumed.

"He wrote that you said you did think of him, all the time," Maroon's daughter continued.

Maroon's wife reflected for a moment before replying, "I do think about my Papa all the time. And he did. I mean, he asked me that just a week or two ago, after he called me in his office."

"He wrote that you cried," Maroon's daughter continued.

Her mom's eyes began to water as she said, "I did cry."

"He wrote that he did, too," Maroon's daughter disclosed.

"Oh?" her mom replied, resuming her lunch preparations while adding, "I didn't notice."

"Mom," her daughter resumed, trying to be sure that her mother was listening, "He wrote that your Papa was in the room crying, too. He wrote that your Papa had asked to see you."

Maroon's wife put down the lunch fixings she had in her hands, to look straight at her daughter, as if trying to be sure that she had heard her daughter correctly. Her daughter simply nodded. But her mother shook her head, saying only, "No."

"Yes, he did," a small voice said from the direction of the bedroom.

Maroon's grandson stood in the hallway outside the bedroom, where he had been listening to his mother and grandmother. His mother and grandmother turned to look at him.

"I didn't see your Papa," Maroon's grandson explained to his beloved Ná, adding, "But I saw others. We played ball with one of them. Mom, you were there."

"It's in the story," Maroon's daughter said quietly to her mother, nodding in corroboration of her son's disclosure. With a tip of head toward her small son, she added, "I didn't see anyone, but he did."

Maroon's wife took a deep breath before returning to her lunch preparations. The little guy turned back to the bedroom, from which the cartoons called.

After a reasonable pause, as she moved the lunch fixings to plates, Maroon's wife asked her daughter, "What are you going to do with the story?"

Maroon's daughter shrugged, saying, "Let's think about it. It's an encouraging story. We could change the names, not of the historical figures but our names. And we could publish it as fiction or mythology. He wrote a lot of both. People would understand."

Maroon's wife pushed a plate across the counter to her daughter, saying, "I made you some anyway. You should eat."

"What about the story, Mom?" Maroon's daughter pressed.

Maroon's wife looked up at her, thinking, before saying, "Do whatever you think."

After lunch, the three of them took a walk through the cemetery. As they embarked, Maroon's wife whispered to her daughter that she didn't want to walk by the gravesite. She needn't have worried. The little guy immediately led them up a dune in the other direction.

For a while, Maroon's daughter kept up with her son, sharing his pretend play, deep and high in the dunes, about great lizards, dragons, and lions. Soon, though, Maroon's daughter tired of the play, letting her son carry on with his own imaginations. Maroon's wife and daughter fell back, walking together while watching the little guy race up and down the dunes, looking for knights, kings, giants, or other subjects and objects of interest.

"You know, he had dementia," Maroon's wife observed in matter-of-fact fashion, referring to her just-departed husband.

"Really?" her daughter replied. After her mother nodded, she added, "Was he doing anything for it?"

Her mother shook her head, replying, "It wasn't the kind you could treat. And he didn't know."

"What do you mean he didn't know?" Maroon's daughter asked with a note of astonishment, adding, "Didn't he go to the doctor? Didn't the doctor tell him?"

"He had labs, ultrasounds, and tests, like we all do at our age," her mother replied, explaining, "The tests must not have been bad enough for the doctor to say anything directly. Unless he kept it from me. But we had authorized each other a long time ago to talk to one another's doctors. And so I called, relating things I was seeing. I then met with his doctor, who said there wasn't much of anything to do but to watch it. We thought it was still early."

Mother and daughter walked on together, daughter calling now and then to her son or replying to her son's shouted inquiries for permission to range farther afield across and up the dunes.

"You know, he died a lot more quickly than we expected," Maroon's wife resumed, adding, "And he didn't show any significant decline until the very end, when he declined so fast."

"It's alright, Mom," her daughter reassured, "You did everything you should have. You were perfect for him."

The two of them stopped and hugged. Maroon's wife cried gently into her daughter's shoulder. Soon, the little guy joined them in a group hug, which he had always loved. Maroon's daughter picked him up so that the three could hold and kiss one another in a long group hug.

"I wish Papa were here for the group hug," the little guy said.

"Just call him," his mother urged.

"Papa!" the little guy called with a laugh, burying his head in his mother and grandmother while wiggling in excitement.

Maroon's daughter soon eased her son back to the ground, having tired of holding him. He was growing. As she did so, though, the little guy whispered to her, "Papa's here."

Maroon's daughter stood erect again. Keeping an encouraging hand on the back of her son, she closed her eyes, took a deep breath, and said quietly in answer to him, "Yes, Papa's here."

Overhearing their exchange, Maroon's wife chimed in, "My Papa's here, too."

"And so are your great knights and kings and giants," Maroon's daughter assured her son.

The three of them soon tired of the walk, turning back toward Maroon's former residence. As they neared the home, Maroon's wife said firmly to her daughter, "Go ahead and publish the story. He'd want us to share it, whether anyone reads it or not. Just be sure that people can take it as real, fictional, or delusion, whichever way they want."

Maroon's daughter smiled back at her mother, nodding and replying, "He'd like that."

"It won't embarrass me, will it?" Maroon's wife asked with a note of caution.

"No, I don't think so, although it depends on how you take it," came her daughter's reply. She added, "And after all, people can take it as fiction. He was a storyteller. But you should read it."

Maroon's wife had already headed up the last stretch to the residence, hustling after her grandson. Without turning back to answer her daughter, she gave a dismissive wave of her hand. Maroon's daughter laughed.

20

Maroon's daughter sat in her car, waiting to meet her son and grandchildren at the playground and small baseball diamond nestled at the base of the dune in the hollow. As Maroon's daughter waited, overlooking the playground above the parking lot, she thought of how many years, decades even, had passed since she had last met her dad Maroon at this same playground, with her little son in tow, just before her dad's passing.

Maroon's daughter remembered how precious it had been to her to see her dad play ball, or try to do so, with his grandson. She also remembered the story she discovered later, attesting to how Maroon and his grandson had hidden help with their play from a Grand Haven native Neal

Ball, born much more than a century earlier. Maroon's daughter had been oblivious to Ball's presence, to the delight of her clever little son.

Her son had grown up long ago, blessed by his Grand Haven community and blessing that same community back by letting it draw richly from him. She was proud of her son for his character, acquired and formed in Grand Haven, including his courage, conviction, sensitivity, insight, and faith. His mother treasured her son's faith above all things, knowing that through it her son would someday join his Papa in the realm beyond, where she, too, would be, much sooner, she hoped and presumed, than her son.

"Beautiful ball field over there," a garrulous voice said to her from the passenger seat of her car.

Maroon's daughter jumped and blanched, seeing the wizened ball player dressed in an old flannel uniform, seated beside her.

"You know, I grew up playing on that field and other fields around town," the ball player said. Interrupting himself, he offered a hand to Maroon's daughter, saying, "I'm sorry. Cornelius Ball. They called me Neal."

Maroon's daughter gave a look of mild alarm at the grizzled hand extended in front of her, causing Ball to pull it sharply back, while saying, "Oh, I'm sorry again. That's a bit forward of me. Look, here's your son and grandchildren. Let's join them."

Indeed, the pickup truck filled with her son and grandchildren had just pulled up beside her car. Ball had already jumped out of her own vehicle, eager to watch the children try their hand at his game on the beautiful diamond. Maroon's daughter made her own way slowly out of her car to greet her son.

"Good day for a little baseball," she greeted her son, who smiled back, while busying himself with getting his two children, a boy and girl, out of their car seats.

"Get the glove and bat out!" Ball urged Maroon's daughter excitedly, referring to Maroon's ancient glove and bat that she had inherited, preserved, and brought along for exactly this occasion.

Maroon's daughter scowled at Ball but dutifully returned to her car to extract the glove and bat from the back.

Ball danced gleefully along as the two grandchildren tumbled out of the truck and down the hill to the playground, nearing the ballfield beyond. Their father, this time oblivious to Ball, when decades earlier he had not been, rushed after his children, trying to corral them in manageable directions.

Maroon's daughter followed at her own slow pace, amused at the cacophony. As she did so, though, she noticed that while her son was unaware of Ball's gamboling presence, her grandchildren were well aware that Ball was there, enjoying their activity. Maroon's daughter smiled and then laughed, thinking how her son had as a little boy seen Ball playing along, while now, as a mature father, he had no vision of the joyful celestial athlete. Apparently, only the very young and old have an affinity for things from the realm beyond.

Maroon's daughter, carrying her dad's old glove and bat, soon caught up with her grandchildren. Handing the ball and bat to her son and pointing to the secluded little diamond, she said, "Teach them to play ball. Over there."

The son accepted the ball and bat and, pointing the bat in the diamond's direction, guided his little boy and girl to the field of play. Ball guffawed at the son's actions, calling him a *knight in shining armor, urging his troops onward.*

"Daddy," the son's little boy called to him as his dad pointed the bat toward the diamond, "You're a knight in shining armor."

The son laughed in response, replying, "Indeed, I am. Onward, my troops, onward!"

When they reached the diamond, Ball took to dashing from home plate to first base and on around second and third toward home. At Ball's urging, the little boy and little girl followed in fits and starts, stopping to examine the bases and anything else of interest along their way. With each pause in their progress, Ball would laugh, carrying on a wildly humorous narrative of their peculiar delays.

"Our hero has paused to examine a beetle!" Ball narrated loudly like a skilled radio announcer, adding after further developments, "But the beetle has expired! Our hero's flight along the base paths has resumed!"

Maroon's daughter initially laughed along with Ball at his antics. But after several strange looks from her son, she tempered her responses to restrained giggles. Her grandchildren also played along to Ball's exaggerated narration. Their dad stood back in amazement at the creativity and joy of their diamond activities, even though they hadn't yet taken the bat or ball. The flannel-uniformed athlete from another century didn't seem to need a bat or ball to stir the children's love for the ballfield.

"Come try the glove," their dad called, holding up Maroon's old glove that his mother had handed to him.

The children raced over, the boy in the lead. He took the glove from his dad, struggling to hold it up as he pulled it awkwardly onto his tiny hand. Ball stood by, laughing at and narrating the boy's unavailing effort. The large and heavy old leather glove hung limply from the boy's hand. When his dad tossed him the ball they had brought along, the boy didn't have the strength or coordination to move the glove anywhere near to catching it.

"You don't need that heavy old glove to play catch," Ball called to the boy, who promptly shook it from his hand, begging his dad to throw the ball to him again. This time, he caught the ball smartly, barehanded.

"See, dad," the boy echoed Ball, "I don't need that heavy old glove."

The same routine ensued with the bat.

As Maroon's daughter watched, remembering the same events occurring between her dad and her son on the same ballfield so long ago, evidently cheered on by Ball then just as now, she wondered with how many children Ball had reenacted the same scene, down through the Grand Haven generations. To how many Grand Haven children had Ball transmitted his joyful spirit of play and his love of sports?

Her remembrance and speculations led Maroon's daughter to wonder how many Grand Haven generations had received similar inspiration in other fields and endeavors from Ferry, Robinson, White, River Woman, Duncan, Loutit, Cutler, Akeley, LaFramboise, and the other historical figures about whom Maroon had written, now so long ago. Surely, their spirits had influenced her, too, as she grew up, studied, married, lived, bore her son, and worked as a teacher in Grand Haven.

Maroon's daughter recalled in particular the incredibly astute and yet remarkably amiable Healy Akeley, the early Grand Haven lawyer-mercantilist who turned his fortune and passion to the highest quality instruction of young women, at a time when that instruction was limited, expensive, and mostly inaccessible, especially in a wilderness frontier. Maroon's daughter, like Akeley, had earned a law degree early in life and had practiced law. But, like Akeley, she had gradually turned her energies to the instruction of young women, with a passion that they and their young male cohorts receive the highest quality education, of the greatest character and in the most-expansive spirit. Grand Haven had blessed her immeasurably, and Grand Haven had drawn from her immeasurably back, after the spirit and model of Healy Akeley.

Surely, these same historic Grand Haven figures had also influenced her son.

As Maroon's daughter watched her son play with his children, joyfully and skillfully aided by Ball, she recalled that her son had been one of the very last children born in Grand Haven. Grand Haven's small hospital, just over the dune east of Maroon's former residence, had announced that it was closing its delivery service. The hospital system that had purchased it was moving all deliveries to larger nearby hospitals in other cities.

Maroon had been present for that birth, just over the dune from his residence. Maroon, his daughter, and his grandson had shared Grand Haven life for too short a period. But Maroon's spirit lived on in his daughter, who transmitted her dad's Grand Haven character and commitments to her son, as her son was now doing for his own children. Maroon's daughter would have had it no other way. She would not have chosen another place in which to receive, share, and transmit the community's spirit.

The games ended with the children exhausted. Ball would have played on. He followed the family to their vehicles, disappointed at their impending departure, imploring Maroon's daughter to return soon. Maroon's daughter smiled at him appreciatively a time or two but avoided speaking to him directly, aware that her son would find it more than peculiar.

With the children safely back in their car seats, water and snacks in hand to mollify them, their young father turned to his mother waiting behind him to say goodbye. Ball looked on.

"This place has blessed us, hasn't it, Son?" Maroon's daughter asked.

He smiled a weak but warm smile. The outing had depleted his own energies, even as it had exhausted his children and mother.

"This place has made you who you are, hasn't it?" Maroon's daughter repeated.

Her son looked humbly down at his hands before looking up to reply, "You made me who you are, you and Papa and Ná."

Maroon's daughter smiled at her son, replying, "And the grand people who made this place, passing along their passionate commitment to its highest ideals and their creator."

Maroon's daughter paused before adding, "Do you remember the ball player you and Papa met here?"

"Remember him?!" her son replied with a big smile and laugh, "He was with me every day as a boy. He's why you and I had so much fun together."

Maroon's daughter stole a glance at Ball, who stood nearby mesmerized at their exchange. A tear rolled down his cheek. Throwing caution to the wind, Maroon's daughter turned to him, bowed briefly in thanks, and then blew him a kiss of appreciation to catch. Ball hilariously jumped for the phantom buss, catching it high over his head, whirling expertly around like an infielder, and tossing it sidearm back to her. Maroon's daughter laughed, while pretending to catch his toss back of her own kiss. Her son shook his head in mock concern and disgust at her inexplicable pantomime.

Maroon's daughter then turned, bid her son goodbye, climbed into her car, and drove off, with a wink and small wave to Ball, who waved back from alongside the parking lot.

Meanwhile, the children's dad stood at his truck's door, fiddling in his pocket for his keys while holding the ball in his other hand. Irritated at not being able to fish the keys out with one hand, he turned toward the playfield from which the family had just come, where Ball stood watching him.

"Here, catch!" the young dad said with a sly smile, suddenly tossing the ball to the astonished flannel-clad player. The young dad laughed, opened the truck door, climbed in, and drove away with a wave to Ball.

www.ingramcontent.com/pod-product-compliance
Lightning Source LLC
LaVergne TN
LVHW041704070526
838199LV00045B/1191